Christian Martenson is an architect living and working throughout the Middle East over the last eighteen years. Christian grew up in the Central Cascade Mountains of the Pacific Northwest in the US, spending much of his time as a back-country sports enthusiast, skiing, hiking, and rock and mountain climbing in the Central, North Cascades, Olympic Peninsula, and British Columbia, Canada. Christian currently lives with his family in Bahrain, and works in Saudi Arabia, but he calls Australia home.

Dedicated to Isaac and Ephraim

CS Martenson

THE BOY AND THE WOLVERINE

AUSTIN MACAULEY PUBLISHERS™

LONDON ∗ CAMBRIDGE ∗ NEW YORK ∗ SHARJAH

ISBN – 9789948834564 – (Paperback)
ISBN – 9789948834557 – (E-Book)

Application Number: MC-10-01-7678815
Age Classification: 17+

Printer Name: iPrint Global Ltd
Printer Address: Witchford, England

First Published (2021)
AUSTIN MACAULEY PUBLISHERS FZE
Sharjah Publishing City
P.O Box [519201]
Sharjah, UAE
www.austinmacauley.ae
+971 655 95 202

I would like to acknowledge my dear friends, Ian McDougall and Ruth Diprose, who challenged and encouraged me to complete my story of *The Boy and the Wolverine*, based on my early years relationship with my grandfather, as an inspiration and encouragement to others who will share in this adventure.

Table of Contents

Preface

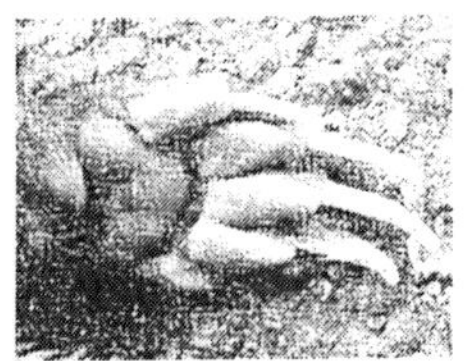

In the forests and above timberline across North America, lives a ferocious carnivore that hunts as a solitary predator, and is seldom seen because of its stealthy and cunning character. The heavy-bodied and short-legged wolverine is known for its legendary refusal to back down in a fight. With strength, shrewdness, and fearlessness, it often challenges animals much larger than itself.

Listening to the legends and the rare stories of encounters with this fearsome creature, could cause the hair on the back of your neck to bristle from fear. But is the wolverine simply a lonely predator with unprecedented ferocity, or is there a mysterious and hidden character to his cunningness that is blended with gentleness, compassion, and a need to belong?

'The Boy and the Wolverine' offers a hidden side of this feared and mysterious creature, and the unusual and yet intimate relationship that grows between the predator and the boy. The deep friendship that develops between these two unlikely characters suggests that even in the midst of fierceness and timidity, is a longing inherent in all creatures for love, kindness, and compassion that overcomes impossible obstacles and creates a mysterious bond. 'The Boy and the Wolverine' reveals how love and compassion in a world that is filled with fear, loneliness, and hopelessness, are more powerful than any fear that we might have of the unknown that often grips us with legendary ferocity or disabling timidity.

Chapter 1
The Far Edge of My Heart

"So, whether on the hilltops high and fair I dwell, or in the
sunless valleys,
Where the shadows lie, what matter? He is there."

It wasn't the first time the boy had been humiliated by being
the last one chosen for one of the teams playing in the
intramural games at school. He was always the first one on
the field, excited with the expectation of playing with his
classmates. However, he was always singled out as the last
kid standing after all his classmates had been selected based
on their ability or their long-standing friendship with the team
captains. But he was OK with this. He had learned to steel
himself against the feelings of embarrassment that seemed to
well up inside him, when the second to the last kid had been
selected and he knew that the game could not begin until he
had been chosen. It wasn't really a selection process anyway;
that ended when the second to the last kid went over to his
team. It seemed to be more of a sympathetic way the other
children had adopted to suppress the embarrassment they felt
for him. He had also learned to find an unusual satisfaction in
this last stage of this selection process that always seemed to
surprise him. The other children attempted to suppress the
embarrassment they felt for the boy. They knew he would be
chosen by the team holding the final selection; however, the
boy always found a mysterious satisfaction in knowing that
the game could not start until this process had been
completed. In this moment, there seemed to be a mysterious
power and control that belonged to him alone. He also knew
that once the game had begun, he had every opportunity to

prove his ability as much as the next boy, or to his greater concern, as much as one of the more athletic girls who had been chosen over him. Nevertheless, his faith in the possibility of exceeding the other children's expectations always bolstered him with determination and enthusiasm, at least for the moment.

The teams were usually well balanced with an equal level of athleticism, except the little the boy brought to his team. And yet, even his mother and grandfather had referred to his natural coordination on regular occasions. In a kindly way, he was always banished to the far-right side of the playing field, both for his own good and the welfare of his team. There was a silent understanding that the team that was left with the boy was compensated with another physically gifted player to compensate for the boy's lack of skill.

The trail to his position at the inside perimeter of the field had become worn by his diligent march every few days at the start and conclusion of the intramural games. And he always took up the same position in the right-hand corner, a few meters from the boundary fence. This was no-man's land, where even the school maintenance workers just left the grass grow unattended. It never saw much sporting activity and the tall grass would quickly impede the roll of any ball, so it was easily retrievable without having to exercise any particular sporting proficiency. And there were also those rare times when the chemistry teacher would blast a soccer ball with determined precision and velocity in his proud display to the older and more attractive senior girls, of his leftover heritage from his playing days at the State University.

The long, wet, and cold winter had given birth to a crisp and fresh early spring morning, with the unmowed grass still heavily laden with dew from the night before. As he made his way to his playing position, his running shoes and socks and his blue denim school pants became soaked up to his knees from the heavy dew collected on the grass overnight. His feet and lower legs began to feel the bite of the cold as the heavy dew seeped into his clothing, little consolation to yet another uneventful intramural game with the Badgers from 7L. He was hopeless in remembering the names given to each of the school teams. He never understood the logic of using native North American forest animals as team names. It seemed more appropriate to use names like the Bullets, Daggers, Rebels, or Bandits, and they were more fitting for a sports team; nevertheless, the banners for the Badgers and Cougars, the Bears, the Beavers, and the Caribou, and the Wolverines decorated the walls of the main hallway through the school. The central corridor connected all of the classrooms to the administrative offices. In his mind, he had named this dreaded section of the school, the gauntlet of shame as he personally referred to it with a grin.

In his short academic career, the main corridor in the school had become a gauntlet he was forced to navigate numerous times every day. Frequently, he found he had to endure emotional and mental anguish, and at times, the insensitive verbal criticism from upper-grade classmates. The central hallway was lined with lockers on either side that created private eddies where students milled around in secret discussions, retrieving books or other paraphernalia from their lockers that they deposited into their schoolbags, preparing for their next class. It had become a proving ground of a kid's popularity, and like many of his other social ventures, he had failed miserably. But then he hadn't really cared that much anyway. There had been the exception of the Japanese girl who had befriended him when he arrived to school the year before on crutches after a skiing accident left him with a torn cartilage in his right leg, requiring a full leg cast. The cast had extended from his ankle to his hip, and seemed to be an over-exaggeration of the surgeon's attempt to immobilize his knee. She had offered to carry his books throughout the two and a half months of his temporary disability and rehabilitation, to allow him to navigate more safely on the wooden crutches supplied by the outpatient clinic. Remarkably, the presence of his new friend at his side created a temporary reprieve from the embarrassment that had become too commonplace as a result of his classmate's comments. Her presence seemed to deflect the deliberate stares from the students in the higher grades that normally would unleash feelings of insecurity and incompetence.

He had been careful not to consider her as a girlfriend, since the disclosure of this amongst his classmates would be emotionally devastating, and would result in relentless teasing. Nevertheless, after the first few weeks of her faithful devotion and growing friendship, his imagination had begun to wonder if he had found what he thought might be true love. But that seemed like another lifetime ago, and after accepting an important position overseas, her father had relocated the family to the Middle East. He often fantasized the possibility of reconnecting with her in another life and finding what his mother often referred to with starry eyes, as a deep and meaningful love relationship that would satisfy the deepest desires of the heart. The greatest desire of his heart, just about every school day though, was simply to get through to the end of class with something of his self-esteem intact, and some sense of accomplishment from his silent efforts.

As soon as he arrived at his field position, he turned around to face his teammates who seemed to be a considerable distance away. He readied himself to observe the start of the game, more as a spectator rather than the actual player he was. He smiled as he noticed that he had cut a long straight swath of a trail through the uncut grass in his march to his playing position. It looked like the wake created by his father's powerboat surging through the water under speed. The glistening dew on the broad strands of grass reflected the morning sun, and reminded him of the froth left in the wake from the twin propellers of his father's Monk-designed cabin cruiser, churning through the water during one of their family's summer cruises in the San Juan Islands. *A special consolation,* he thought, *to share with no one in particular, but nevertheless, an encouraging thought just the same.*

There was a slight breeze blowing across the field from the northeast, carrying the faint yet distinctive fragrance of Douglas fir and cedar from the forest that began a short distance behind the school's maintenance buildings. The forest had become a mystical retreat for the boy as far back as he could remember, when he was allowed to accompany his grandfather in search of firewood during the changing autumn months, in preparation for the long, cold winter. He fondly remembered their adventurous sorties into the deep woods after the forest had been transformed by the heavy snowfall after winter had finally arrived. He remembered how his grandfather had taught him to crush the dark green needles from the cedar to create the wonderful fragrance locked away in the needles. The residue would remain on his fingers the entire day, and he was reminded of this secret of the forest every time he raised his hand and smelled the gentle and lasting natural scent of the tree. He also remembered how his grandfather tried to explain to him what he referred to as the symbolism of life: that there was a mysterious relationship between the fragrance from the crushed needles of the cedar, and the adversities of human life that emitted a special fragrance in the character of a person. As much as he tried to understand what his grandfather meant, it remained hidden and only registered a small grin, as he pondered the ridiculousness of comparing life to crushed cedar needles.

When he and his grandfather first began their retreats into the forest, he felt his grandfather had simply tolerated his presence. After all, it was one of the few times his grandfather could enjoy smoking the long, thick cigars that he savored. He suffered loving abuse from his grandmother or anyone else who considered the repulsive cigar smoke throughout the house. But as they ventured into the forest, the smell of his cigar always took on quite a different fragrance. The distinctive smell provided a compass-like indicator back to his grandfather's side, after his numerous adventures exploring the meandering tracks left in the snow by a small animal in search of food. Occasionally, he was awarded the discovery of the tracks of a much larger animal that had ventured down from the base of the Eastern Ridge. His grandfather had a great love for the outdoors and especially the mountains. His initial attitude of tolerance grew into a sense of companionship, and eventually an intimate friendship between the two of them. His grandfather took delight in imparting what seemed to be a wealth of knowledge, respect, and appreciation for the forest and mountains that had saturated his soul as a hunting guide in the Alaskan wilderness many years earlier. He had relished the rare occasion when alerting his grandfather to a recent discovery of large unrecognizable animal tracks, his grandfather would quickly come to his side, and with a grin from ear to ear and adventure glistening in his eyes, he would carefully scrutinize the tracks left in the snow. After a few moments of thoughtful analysis, with great pride and self-assurance, his grandfather would identify the tracks of the animal, and include a detailed description of the animal's weight, physical condition, and temperament. The boy was always fascinated how his grandfather could glean so much information about the animal from a few tracks left in the snow. He challenged his grandfather on this matter numerous times, but his grandfather always referred to his keen tracking sense as a special gift he had inherited from his own mother after a romantic fling she presumably had with a young Nooksack Indian chieftain. Taking his grandfather's head in his hands and drawing him as close as possible, he studied his facial features very carefully, but could never detect these unique Indian traits for himself.

There were also those times when the boy would feign the discovery of strange animal tracks of some mysterious and ferocious animal that he masterfully created in the snow. Calling his grandfather to share in his discovery and identify the animal, his grandfather would very politely go through his antics of analysis. After a few quiet moments studying the tracks, he would rise up from his haunches, and smelling the light breeze and looking off into the forest beyond, would quietly suggest that the tracks appeared to belong to those of the feared wolverine, letting the name linger on the breeze for the longest of times. He would then break the silence in resuming his normal voice and announce that he was probably mistaken though, and cantor off to resume his place on the trail. The boy was left to study his own invention to make sure he had not mistaken his own creation for those of an actual animal during the short time his eyes were following his grandfather's movements to the place of his feigned discovery.

The boy's playing position also afforded him a wonderful view of the rugged granite peaks beyond the forest that were still encased in a fabric of snow and ice after a harsh winter. The slight northeasterly breeze he felt blowing across the field, was being transformed on the mountain above into a strong and bitterly cold wind. He watched with fascination the windblown snow that resembled the vapor trail of a high-altitude jet on its lonely flight to some unknown destination, being swept over the top of the serrated summit ridge. The boy remembered that while early spring seemed to have arrived and the morning sun began to warm his face, the muddied water in the holes left in the streets covered by a thick layer of ice was still an indicator that nighttime temperatures were still very much a part of winter. He remembered his grandfather's teaching that to be caught out in the forest or mountains unprepared, could mean a quick experience with hypothermia. His grandfather enjoyed expounding on what he considered to be the most effective remedy against hypothermia. He was a strong advocate of cohabiting a goose-down sleeping bag with a friend, or in the boy's case, his sister, to allow the dead air space inside the sleeping bag to be heated by the two bodies close together as a means of warding off the effects of hypothermia. In his opinion, his grandfather's recommendation against hypothermia might be acceptable with consenting adults; however, he remained convinced that freezing to death was a preferred option over sharing a goose-down sleeping bag with his younger sister.

He was roused out of his daydreaming stupor by one of the more athletic girls on his team yelling at the top of her voice that the game had finished, and that it was time to return to class. His time 'in the field,' as his teammates referred to it, always seemed to go very fast when he dwelled on other things that held a fascination and intrigue. The other option was to become burdened with the mundane and often times hurtful things that seemed to fill his life, which was really never an option out in no-man's land. And he always looked forward to the special visitor time in class that followed the intramural games, when one of the prominent adults from the community would share some tale of adventure that always captured his imagination. And there were also the local heroes from the police and fire or mountain rescue team who would paint a colorful picture of their daily life, changing the boy's career aspirations for the moment. His alleged lack of athletic prowess and what many thought to be his low self-esteem, never damped his vibrant imagination or his sensitivity to what his grandfather called 'the things of the spirit,' whatever that was supposed to mean. He accepted this as a compliment and felt some degree of pride with his grandfather's accolades, even though he didn't understand it himself, nor was able to explain its meaning to anyone else.

Chapter 2
Survival of the Fittest

"Small was my faith, should it weakly falter now that the lupine have ceased to blow; frail was the trust that now should alter, doubting His love when storm clouds grow."

It had been a bitterly cold and grueling long winter for the young wolverine. His mother had fallen pregnant the summer before to a dominant older male from the northern ranges that had singled her out during the height of the mating season. He was easily thirty to forty percent larger than his mother, and had overpowered the younger males of the pack in an uncontested aggressive one-sided physical encounter. His mother quickly learned that submission to her stronger male counterpart was her best defensive strategy to prevent serious injury. After their mating ritual, he then challenged the leader of the pack in a fight to the death that quickly resulted in his father taking command of the leadership of the pack. He dethroned the leader's lifeless body that remained in the tangled brier and undergrowth that he had been backed into before suffering a fatal blow. The scavengers of the forest wasted no time in reducing the body to skeletal remains overnight.

She had given birth to a litter of three the following spring, with the young wolverine being born as the smallest of the kits. He learned very quickly, even during the early spring months when food seemed to be plentiful and the high alpine meadows had become a spectacular mass of alpine flowers including lupines, paintbrushes, and crocuses, that survival was paramount. The kits had developed rapidly throughout the spring and summer months. They had grown up to half their adult size by the time winter had blown in with fury and the first heavy snowfall had transformed the alpine meadows and the area above timberline into a barren white landscape. Unlike many of the other forest animals, the wolverine does not hibernate in the late fall through winter, and their burrow had become a safe and protected haven to endure the winter storms.

The wolverines were characterized by a large stocky body, bushy tail, dark fur, short legs, and broad, webbed feet with long, sharp claws on the front feet and furry soles. His father had taught them his strategies of hunting, although most of their food source came from the carrion left by the pack of timber wolves that lived on the Eastern Ridge about two kilometers away. *Much too close for comfort,* he had thought, but his father's tactic in positioning their burrow so close to the dangerous wolf pack, had also ensured abundant food for the pack throughout the harsh winter.

Apart from the wolf pack, the wolverines feared no other predator and were quite capable of attacking most animals much larger than themselves, including the large bull moose that had wandered below timberline in early spring. His father had caught the scent of the moose long before the bull had come into view. After a considerable time of stealthy movement through the upper forested area, his father spied the moose grazing on an outcropping of lush vegetation that had been protected throughout the winter by about a meter of snow. The grass and alpine flowers underneath the blanket of snow had begun to climb heavenward in response to the warmth of the sun, as the snowfields began to melt off. The moose had descended below timberline to satisfy his great hunger that remained after foraging for scant amounts of food throughout the ruthless winter. This proved to be his fatal mistake. The moose was completely exposed on the small island of vegetation surrounded by patches of deeper snow that had melted and frozen numerous times over the winter months, and resembled dirty concrete. The wolverine's appearance resembles a small bear with its short legs and long, bushy tail. Its running action, if you can call it that, is a very unusual and distinctive hopping motion, with its back hunched over and a side and front-over gait. His father's physical appearance may not have made much of an impression with the young bull, when the scent merged with vision and he turned to face his foe, although he was still about sixty meters from the outcropping.

The moose's shoulder height measured almost eight feet and his long bulbous snout produced a defiant warning blast. He turned to stand his ground towards what appeared to be the wolverine's position that was still indistinguishable amongst the stand of cedar. The bell or loose piece of skin under the bull's throat swayed back and forth as he moved his massive head slowly, raising his snout to search the crisp spring air for a more recognizable scent of the intruder downwind. He nearly missed the very slight lateral movement of the dull yellow stripe along the wolverine's side, against the dark green cedar branches that had been pushed down by the weight of the snow throughout the winter. The low hung branches provided effective camouflage. He had glanced ever so briefly at the Mountain Chickadee that had drawn attention to itself by its shrill chattering, perched in one of the cedar branches directly above the wolverine.

The bull moose had shed his antlers during the winter, and the markings of his new antlers' growth were erupting on the top of his head. When fully developed by mid-summer, they would measure five to six feet across, and weigh up to eighty-five to ninety pounds. The moose's shoulders were well developed, forming his characteristic hump, and he was equipped with long legs and broad hooves that allowed him to walk efficiently through deep snow. However, his father's powerful and rapid hopping movement had enabled him to quickly cover the short distance between them as he effortlessly powered through the deep snow. The young bull was determined to stand his ground, and pivoted around to face his attacker, relying on his strong front and hind legs as lethal weapons. However, the moose had been caught off guard by underestimating the quickness of the wolverine as he rapidly closed the gap between them. His father's last powerful hop had launched him from the edge of the snow in an upward thrusting lunge into the underside of the bull's throat. The bull moose heard the final warning chatter from the Mountain Chickadee, as the wolverine's massive jaw and razor-sharp teeth ripped open his throat. A moment later, the bull crashed to the ground, crumpling the delicate paintbrush and lush alpine grass he had been grazing on an instant earlier under his body, as he exhaled his last breath. The moose provided a protein-rich food source for the kits and the other members of the pack, and earned his father even greater esteem as a clever and cunning hunter in addition to his dominant leadership role.

The only other predator the wolverines feared were the dangerous and mysterious humans. Men would hunt the wolverines for their long coarse fur with its ability to shed moisture, making it frost-resistant, and prized as trim for hoods, and lining for parkas.

An unusual fear had been instilled in the young wolverine when the pack had witnessed the kill of one of his mother's sisters in late fall before the first snow. A group of hunters had tracked the wolverine pack for three days. The first .338 bullet from the .30 caliber magnum rifle had been a lethal shot, but three shots later, she was finally fallen in the thick undergrowth of the forest in a futile attempt to escape her predators, while the pack escaped to the backside of the ridge. The hunters seemed to be satisfied with their trophy since after three days of lying in wait, the scent and signs of the hunters had disappeared altogether. The pack had returned to the last known location of his mother's sister's warm body; however, only a few tuffs of gray silky fur remained as a memorial to her death. The young wolverine's fear had been fueled by the fact that apart from the loud crack of the rifle's blast that echoed across the ranges, and the almost unintelligible dull thud from the .338 bullet that had found its mark an instant later, there had been no visual presence of the hunters, just the slightest disturbance of scent in the air that alerted the pack to the impending danger.

Spring had been a time of uninhibited frolicking with his siblings and other young wolverines in the pack. The young males shared the added privilege of accompanying their fathers and the older males on hunting sorties into the dense forest, and oftentimes to timberline in search of larger prey. The older males relied on their incredible sense of smell to identify small prey, which was their staple diet, and rarely hunted anything half their size. However, occasionally, the hunting pack would work together to hunt larger prey such as the mountain goats that inhabited the areas above timberline. Occasionally, the goats descended to eat from the alpine fields that made them an easy target. His mother and the other females of the pack remained in the den tending to the younger kits. He was pleased he had been accepted as a full-fledged member on the hunting trips, although his initial contribution to the food supply seemed to have been wrought with delays due to his smaller stature. He found that the intimidation he had sensed from the other males, thwarted his confidence and ability. Nevertheless, he was determined that his unusual cunning and hunting prowess, that seemed to be a trait he had inherited from his father, would compensate for any misgivings about his size.

The spring had quickly changed into the warm early weeks of summer, and he had taken great interest in the mating ritual between the males and females during the first months of summer. He was quite surprised how submissive the females had become, including his own sister who had attempted on numerous times to force her supremacy over her smaller sibling. He was also fascinated with the comical display of arrogance and dominance the older males displayed as they selected for themselves one of the more submissive females, who may have been exerting her dominance over her male suitor only weeks earlier. Needless to say, he was quite confused when his sister, who had nipped one of his mother's sister's older male siblings and regularly forced him to cower under her more aggressive play, willingly submitted to what appeared to be his feigned display of fierce aggression. The first few months of summer seemed to fly past with a growing anticipation of expectancy, as the first kits were born and the pack became a buzz of activity.

Compared to the much more masculine male wolverines, the kits were born with very little fur, and were kept warm during the cooler nights by both parents. While they could see and walk, they did neither until they grew enough fur to survive the colder nighttime temperatures. Summertime in the forest could still unleash a violent storm, transforming the area above timberline into a white snow-covered landscape. He also noticed that a number of the newly born litters appeared to decrease in size rapidly after some of the smaller kits had died from exposure during a summer storm, as nighttime temperatures hovered around freezing. He had been fortunate that his smaller size had not discouraged either one of his parents, especially his father, from leaving him to die. They had cared for all of the siblings without partiality. He was also intrigued the way the young kits were kept warm in their concealment within their mother's large pouch on her belly, that amazingly seemed to be able to accommodate the entire litter if required. Like himself, each of the kits was expected to contribute to the pack. If they were unwilling or unable to do so, they were left behind to die, and their final resting place the day before was barren a day later after the scavengers of the forest had made quick work of their lifeless body.

The pack began to grow to twice its original population following the birth of over twelve litters of rapidly developing kits with hungry mouths. The young wolverine had begun to successfully apply his cunning and shrewd hunting skills. He enjoyed continuing success in catching small rodents, rabbits, and a white-tailed fawn. These had been his first real test of his smaller stature. He had also successfully hunted a marmot and a goat that had literally dropped out of the sky like manna from heaven.

He had been hunting an older, more mature marmot for the last two to three hours at timberline, and was determined that the marmot's cunning and slyness would not outwit his own craftiness and perseverance. The marmot's brownish fur allegedly provided him effective camouflage against potential predators amongst the rock fall at the bottom of the ridge. The marmot had remained motionless as the young wolverine moved past catching the scent of the marmot and the undeniable smell of its thick, wet fur about a hundred meters down wind. He had missed detecting the marmot amongst the brownish igneous rock in the rock fall. He was about fifty meters past the marmot when the marmot let off a loud whistle to communicate to its siblings above the impending danger and the approaching predator. The young wolverine chased the marmot into a narrowing rock crevice, large enough to accommodate the marmot but too small to allow the young wolverine to enter. He camped out on top of the opposite boulder thinking to outwait the marmot. This proved to be futile, and just when he had decided to abandon the hunt and return to the pack, the marmot made a run for the next crevice, following a series of hidden passages between the rocks that provided safety from predators. The wolverine's perseverance was fueled by the thought that the marmot, being a creature of habit, very likely would attempt another move to the next crevice, as he sought safe passage down through the rock fall. As soon as the marmot buried himself in the second crevice, the wolverine did a reconnoiter of the surrounding area. He discovered what appeared to be the only option available to the marmot if he was going to continue his descent below the timberline and the safety of his well-protected burrow hidden amongst the dense undergrowth of the forest at the toe of the rock fall. Instead of camping out on the opposite boulder this time, the wolverine took up his position to the right of the entrance to the marmot's hiding place, but outside the line of sight.

Once again, the marmot's patience and perseverance to outwait the wolverine tried him to near breaking point. The smooth form of the large boulder the wolverine had perched himself on had been exposed to the sun for most of the day. The warmth from the rock and the gentle breeze whispering through the cedars, lulled him into a sleepy stupor. The awakening blast of falling rock that had been dislodged from the ridge above collided with the rock fall below, sending shards of rock whizzing past him, and filling the air with a stench of sulfur. He was quickly brought back to his senses as he focused on the falling rock further up the rock fall. He immediately spied the marmot cautiously emerging through a narrow chimney that exited at the top of the boulder. The wolverine noticed that the marmot was preparing to make a final dash to the crevice he had staked out and was guarding. With renewed agility and speed, the marmot unsuspectingly dashed right into the wolverine, toppling both of them off the backside of the boulder to the ground about a meter below. In mid-air and in a split second, the wolverine had fastened his massive jaws around the marmot's neck, and the marmot's lifeless body now lay next to the wolverine at the base of the boulder. The hype of activity and exertion of the short one-sided battle in just a few seconds had tired the young wolverine, and he found comfort on a clump of worn alpine grass at the base of the boulder where he was able to lay and recover his energy.

No sooner had his breathing assumed a more normal rhythm, when he was startled by a loud thud about two meters behind him with a small ground tremor. The air surrounding him was immediately saturated with the smell of a young goat that had ventured too close to the precipice above. The goat had ventured too near the edge, and losing his footing, plunged over the seventy-five-meter cliff face to the rocks below. The lifeless eyes of the young male goat stared back at him with no recognition of the ferocious predator standing within striking distance of his prey. The goat had met his end when he collided with the granite overhang that projected out halfway down the cliff face. There was little the wolverine had to do apart from ferrying his game back to the pack, which proved to be far more exhausting than his hunting expedition. His ambiguous description of the hunting tactics he had employed to be rewarded so abundantly were thankfully lost in the praise and accolades he received from his mother and father and the other males of the pack.

Chapter 3
Into the Wilderness

"Great is the easy conqueror; yet the one who is wounded sore, breathless, all covered o'er with blood and sweat, sinks fainting, but fighting evermore – is greater yet."

The long warm days of autumn began to change with a crisp coolness in the early morning as the leaves on the maples turned blood-red, and variations of purple and the Mountain Aspen and other deciduous trees began to drop their leaves, creating soft carpeting throughout the forest. The damp decomposing leaves on the forest floor also provided excellent stealth for the young wolverine in his continuing success as a respected hunter amongst the pack.

The young wolverine had grown nearly to his adult size and weight, and he had proved himself beyond any doubt amongst the other males of the pack that he had indeed inherited his father's hunting and leadership skills. However, his smaller stature continued to plague his credibility of any future aspirations he sought for following in his father's dominance in the pack. There was a hype of activity throughout the forest as summer moved into autumn and fall and the smaller animals and larger bears began preparing their dens and winter retreats to hibernate throughout the harsh winter. This left many of the smaller animals that provided the staple diet for the wolverine pack, exposed as they scurried to collect and store sufficient food reserves to last the winter months. The wolverine's hunting strategies also had to be carefully adjusted to avoid the wolf pack from the Eastern Ridge that had begun to expand their hunting territory as prey became less plentiful above timberline.

The timber wolves, or gray wolves as they were typically referred to, also suffered the same fate as the wolverines through their encounters with humans. Human encroachment had reduced the population of their pack; however, through the spring and summer months, the wolf pack, like the wolverines, had grown twice-fold. The concern of this predator to the wolverine pack, especially during the winter months, registered more as a sense of suppressed anxiety initially, with his father and the other older males of the pack. A lone wolf by itself did not represent too much of a threat to a wolverine or the pack. However, the wolves were apex predators throughout their territorial range, with only humans and an occasional angry grizzly bear posing any significant threats to them. And the timber wolves were very much social predators that both lived and hunted in nuclear families as a pack. Their primary food source were ungulates or hoofed animals like the moose and elk, the bison in the lower open areas, the deer, and as the opportunity presented itself, the wolverine and smaller forest animals.

The wolf pack was well aware of the presence of the wolverines about two kilometers from their Eastern Ridge home where they had lived over the last few years; however, the wolves had enjoyed the same abundance of prey and food that the wolverines had experienced throughout the spring and summer months. The wolverines give off a very strong, extremely unpleasant odor from their anal glands, giving rise to their nickname 'skunk bear,' and this was easily detectable by the wolves, even two kilometers away in their home.

The days and nights continued to cool and the northeasterly winds that brought the bitter cold of winter began to build much earlier. And then within a single day, the first winter storm unleashed its fury in mid-October, and the forest was once again transformed into a white wilderness with the area above timberline resembling a harsh icy desert that appeared desolate overnight. The abundance of food in late autumn had disappeared altogether, and the male hunting pack expanded their hunting sorties to the lower forested areas below the Eastern Ridge.

During one early-morning hunting sortie, the wolverines spied a deer with its fawn just below timberline. The deer instantly smelled the wolverine's unpleasant odor, and realizing the presence of a predator and the impending danger, began to flee into the protection of the forest. The hunting pack gave chase and within half an hour, the tiring deer was overcome by two of the stronger males who had outpaced the remainder of the pack and made the kill. The hunters had been away from their home for three days, and the deer and its fawn provided much-needed food for energy and to curb their hunger that had begun to cloud their better judgment. The pursuit of the deer and its fawn had also brought them dangerously close to the flanks of the Eastern Ridge, where the wolf pack had dug in during the early winter storm.

The scent of the large male timber wolves was completely unintelligible even to the wolverines. The young wolverine's cunning sense had alerted him to a potential danger and threat, although there was still no visual recognition to this effect, as he slowly backed away from the deer and its fawn that the other males of the hunting party were consuming, to scan the surrounding terrain. Something was different. The snowy forest and what had been turned into a white desert above timberline seemed to have the same monotonous appearance as it had the last three days; however, something was out of place. His father had felt the same uneasiness, and had also backed away from the kill. The two of them carefully scrutinized every tree including the boulders above timberline that had deposited themselves in the rock fall from the Eastern Ridge above, and were covered with a dusting of fresh snow from the storm the night before. With raised heads, they both scented the air and detected the smell of the timber wolves at the same time. A moment later, three powerfully built animals with large, deeply descending ribcages and sloping backs, quietly emerged from behind a stand of Douglas Fir, assuming a defensive position, aligned breast to breast. The wolf's abdomens were pulled in and their necks appeared heavily muscled. All three of them had large heavy heads with wide foreheads, strong jaws, and long blunt muzzles. Their ears were relatively small and triangular with their heads raised in a position of alertness. The wolverines were all too familiar with the cunning and physical prowess of this predator and the danger a wolf pack represented to them. They were also very aware of the wolf's capacity to run at speeds of fifty-five kilometers per hour for up to twenty minutes, which was no match for the wolverine's unusual hopping gait. The three timber wolves appeared as fearless threesome predators silently studying the male wolverine's hunting pack consuming its prey. His father had assessed the impending danger even before the cloud of vapor from the crisp morning air had formed from his second breath. The other males recognized the concern in their leader, and slowly released their portion of the kill. In what appeared to be a rehearsed escape strategy, all of them, with the exception of his father, turned and fled the scene of the kill in a well-choreographed dash into the dense part of the forest and back down the trail. Unbeknown to the young wolverine, his father had caught the scent of the additional ten male timber wolves while they were still hidden from view, but as the wolf pack assembled together about fifty to sixty meters upwind of the wolverines, his father realized the sacrificial act he had been forced into. His primary focus had quickly changed to safeguard the fleeing males, and ensure the welfare and safety of the entire wolverine pack two kilometers away, who remained completely unaware of the events that were poised to commence in the next moment, events that would forever alter the wolverine pack and have a profound impact on the younger wolverine.

Spurred on by hunger and their intense rage that another predator had trespassed into their territory they had claimed and marked repeatedly for themselves, the wolf pack descended upon the remaining wolverine leader as he stood his ground against hopeless odds. He knew that the ferocity that he was displaying in his defensive posture, and his growl that ordinarily would send shivers down the spine of most prey, would do little to deter the attacking wolves. His final sacrificial act of his life had been intended to temporarily draw the attention of the wolf pack to himself, to buy enough time for the other males, including his offspring, to rescue the remaining females and kits in the wolverine pack below, allowing them to make an immediate escape to safety. However, he had underestimated the timber wolves' own shrewdness and cunningness as five of the wolves fell off from the pack's surge, and surrounded him in what would become his last stand to the death. The remaining eight wolves did not even break their cadence as they sped past him in their deathly pursuit of the other males to protect their territorial rights and secure an abundance of food by decimating the remaining wolverine pack.

The wolverine leader fought valiantly as he mortally wounded one of the wolves with a crushing bite that punctured the wolf's neck. The wolf cowered away to die a painful death amongst the undergrowth. However, it was impossible to protect every side as the four remaining wolves upheld a vicious attack at both sides, and in front and behind the wolverine. He had become disoriented very quickly, attempting to protect all sides, and having lost considerable blood from strategically delivered bites from the wolves. It was simply a matter of time before his reserves of energy were fully depleted and the largest male of the remaining four wolves locked his massive jaws around the wolverine's neck. Death came quickly as his last thoughts were of the welfare of the pack. He was wounded sore, breathless, and covered with blood and sweat, and was quickly fainting but bravely fighting on, even in his death.

The young wolverine had maintained the same frantic pace of the larger males as they raced back to the pack to sound the alarm, and quickly organize an immediate escape into the dense part of the forest where they might have a fighting chance against the wolf pack. A mental imprint of his father's sacrificial stand against the wolves was etched on his mind. The impact that the loss of his father had on him to such a cruel and vicious death had been only a fleeting thought at the moment though. His immediate focus was on himself and the other male wolverines reaching the females and 'kits' and the few males who had remained behind in their home before the wolves descended upon them.

The two-kilometer run to the wolverines' home would have normally taken up to thirty minutes through the dense forested undergrowth or perhaps forty-five minutes skirting timberline; however, at their present pace, they had covered three-fourths of the distance in a little over fifteen minutes. Their thick fur was soaked with sweat and matted with debris from the undergrowth that had splintered from passing tree limbs and lodged in their fur like a forest decoration. The young wolverine quickly decided against a momentary halt to their frantic escape to evaluate the position of the wolves. He could hear the crashing and breaking of tree limbs only a short distance behind them, created by the descending wolf pack that had abandoned any efforts of maintaining stealth. As they quickly drew near to the pack's home, it became apparent to the young wolverine and the other males that an immediate about-turn to face the vicious wolf pack in what would become their own sacrificial death, was their only option to safeguard the unsuspecting pack below. Their arrival into the midst of the wolverines' encampment would be a certain sentence of slaughter at the merciless savagery of the angry wolf pack.

A slight widening of the trail immediately before the denser portion of the forest that led into the wolverines' territorial enclave, provided the male hunting packs last option to take their stand against the wolves. The high side of the trail was bordered by a moderate rise of rock fall that continued to the base of the ridge high above. Heavy undergrowth had grown up through the rocks, and numerous fallen and rotting trees had been blown over during winter storms from years past. The undergrowth had engulfed the trees in their final resting places which had become home to a plethora of insects and the occasional small forest animals. The lower side of the trail steeply fell away to a ravine, and a mountain creek below that became a thunderous torrent during the spring thaw and summer rains. It had been reduced to a barely audible babble of water with ice and snow covering most of the narrow ravine. There was no apparent way around the main trail, and in what appeared like a well-designed movement, all of the male wolverines turned on the approaching wolf pack at the same time in what they knew would be their final stand.

The widening of the trail provided only enough room for the seven remaining wolverines, stacked breast to breast to confront the wolf pack. Their strategy was limited to creating more of a barricade to slow the descending wolf pack then to wound and dispel their attackers in their characteristic defensive fighting technique. Their final display of courage and aggression did little to slow the attacking wolves who had gained considerable momentum, as the trail descended to the lower elevations through the forest.

Unlike the wolverine, the timber wolf will never back down from a fight. Wolves are very skilled fighters, even attacking each other in order to determine the alpha male or leader of the pack. The wolf would most likely initiate the fight, as it is a determined killer and will try to kill and eat anything. The wolves' strategy would be to attempt to bite the neck of the wolverines, and hang on until its death. The relentless wolf will continue to press the fight as the wolverines tried to escape. The slightest hesitation or wavering of commitment to the fight by the wolverines would tip the scales very quickly to the wolves' advantage.

The attacking wolves had no regard for the wolverines' stand of defiance or their display of aggression. The about-face tactic by the wolverines seemed to further incite the wolf pack as they accelerated their vicious pursuit and plowed into the wolverines with their massive shoulders as ramrods, bowling over three of the seven wolverines, sending them careening down the steep sides of the ravine into the icy waters of the creek below. The remaining four wolverines, including the young wolverine who had quickly followed in his father's heritage assuming the role of dominant leader, were sadly no match for the eight wolves. Two of the older wolverines were very quickly disposed of with a fatal bite to the neck and abdomen, and discarded into the undergrowth above the trail. They would be consumed later and provide food reserves for the wolf pack and the young cubs in their dens back on the Eastern Ridge. The young wolverine with his sister's mate at his side, proved their bravery and strength pitted with impossible odds against the unrelenting wolves. Two of the savage wolves attacked his sister's mate from two sides, puncturing his throat and opening his abdomen in a mortal wound, but he continued to defend his position and faithfulness to the young wolverine leader in his death. Realizing that the one wolverine had been mortally wounded, the remaining wolves concentrated their full attack on the young wolverine leader. His comrade in battle, who was wounded sorely, silently crawled into the undergrowth of the embankment at the high side of the trail, with his breathing becoming increasingly labored. A moment later, his lifeless eyes stared out at the continuing battle between the wolves and the young wolverine.

The wolves had inflicted wounds on the legs and back of the young wolverine, but his quickness because of his smaller stature had spared him any mortal blow from the powerful crushing jaws. He had never experienced such strength in an opponent, and his fear fueled his determination to be victorious in the battle. But even in his unprecedented display of bravery, his chances of survival rapidly diminished as the four wolves who had remained behind to dispose of his father, joined the attack. The adrenalin pumping through his body masked the excruciating pain that was beginning to rise up from strategic bites delivered over his body by one of the larger males. His aggressive breathing pattern in the battle began to change involuntarily to increasingly labored breathing, in what seemed to be the remaining moments of his life. A second wolf leveraged the young wolverine's body completely off the ground with a second-deep bite to the nape of his neck. The wolf's teeth cutting into his flesh and the brute strength of his attacker, lifted him up off the trail and tossed him over the edge towards the ravine. He tumbled down the steep embankment through the undergrowth towards the creek below. The low-lying branches from the small trees growing on the steep sides of the ravine inflicted numerous open cuts as he hurled past. Splinters from the branches of the trees penetrated his thick fur and skin like a hundred daggers. His body collided with a granite slab jutting out from the steep slope ten meters above the bottom of the ravine, catapulting him airborne the remaining descent into the icy creek. He landed with a dull thud and splash as his backside and legs plunged into the icy water, and his upper body collided with the snow-covered rubble along the creek, knocking the wind out of his lungs. A dark cloud quickly began to envelope him as he fought to retain consciousness. He began to shiver uncontrollably from his immersion into the icy water as the first stages of shock from loss of blood began to slow all of his bodily functions. He willed himself to drag his body out of the creek onto a small grassy area on the opposite side of the ravine, concealed from the trail above by a large rotting cedar. The grassy bed had been protected from the heavier snowfall by a canopy of low-hanging branches from a stand of cedars that had survived the early winter storm. The small grassy spot had a light dusting of snow, and provided camouflage behind the cedar log from the astute sight of any returning wolves who would be scavenging the site of the battle for the lifeless bodies of their opponents. He had often thought about this moment, and how his life would end as he curled up to try to generate warmth with his remaining reserves as his final battle with the elements began to weaken him. He knew he had fought gallantly and that even in death, his father would have been proud of him. The forest grew still around him as he heard the faint yelps of the 'kits' and the remaining wolverines in the pack in the distance, being savaged by the marauding wolves. His breathing continued to slow and become more labored as exhaustion from the battle consumed him. His eyes slowly gave in to the struggle of remaining open, and in what appeared to be his final moments of life, he lay motionless as a shroud of deep and dark sleep began to enclose around him.

Chapter 4
An Unusual Discovery

"A voice as bad as conscience rang interminable changes in one everlasting whisper day and night repeated – so: something hidden. Go and find it. Go and look behind the ranges – something lost behind the ranges, lost and waiting for you – go!"

The early winter storm was a welcomed relief to the boy, with a fall of up to twelve inches of snow overnight. The cedar logs that he and his grandfather had cut earlier in the fall, crackled loudly and burned hot in the open fireplace as he listened carefully with his mother to the long list of school closures being reported on the radio.

The winter storm the night before had transformed the beauty of the late fall. The ground that had been covered in a sea of leaves and the remaining leaves on the trees that were turning vivid colors of yellow, ochre, violet, and blood-red, had been changed dramatically into a barren white landscape. The heavy covering of snow on the ground created a still quietness that the boy always found unique to the winter. The varied sounds of the day seemed to be muffled, and there was a quiet peace that came with the blanket of snow. And then it came – the name of his school reported with the closures of the other schools throughout the district. His anxiety immediately turned to joy, with the report of his school now closed due to the winter snowstorm overnight. He felt a sense of relief as well when he realized that his school's closure also provided him the reprieve and additional time to complete the geography assignment, he had procrastinated in starting earlier in the week. The heavy snowfall overnight gave birth to a new day that forced schedules and agendas for the day to be changed or postponed. The normal attitudes of tolerance, suppressed anxiety, and stress, in anticipation of the challenges and disappointments of the day, disappeared and a feeling of peace and cheerfulness seemed to be shared by everyone. The falling snow had momentarily been suspended as if to allow the new day to emerge; however, the regular updates, also reported on the radio by the weather service, predicted continuing snowfall for the next few days with heavier falls expected overnight, as the temperature dropped below freezing. He knew from the previous year that extended school closures during late fall and through the winter would also reduce his summer holiday time, but that was still months away, and his vision for his academic career at the moment was based on a day-to-day perspective.

A heavy rap at the backdoor caused the double-glazed window panel in the center of the door to shudder, signaling his grandfather's arrival. The boy's concentration on listening to the report of school closures had preoccupied his thoughts completely. He had not allowed himself the luxury of considering much more exciting opportunities that the snowfall and school closures would offer for the day, until he was assured that he could legitimately miss school. After all, true to her own admonition, Mrs. Imus was a hard task master when it came to schoolwork and the timely submission of assignments. He half expected she would have cut a deal with the weather bureau to include with their report, an update for all students of hers from 8L, to make sure their geography assignments were dutifully handed in before the close of school, so she could review them and be able to post individual grades the following Monday. But the beauty of the winter storm that left a heavy deposit of snow everywhere, had the power to completely alter the disciplined work ethic of even Mrs. Imus.

The backdoor flew open, revealing Grandfather as if he had just returned from Northern Alaska and one of his hunting trips to the Brooks Range in mid-winter, leading a hunting expedition in search of caribou and elk. His tall frame had lost much of its muscle tone and bulk since his days as an Alaskan hunting guide, accomplished cross-country skier, and avid mountaineer. And his red and black checkered woolen shirt that had been purchased from the local hunting outfitter, perhaps twenty years earlier, hung loose on his diminishing frame. He was dressed in the same old gray and brown loose-fitting woolen knickers that Grandmother had repaired countless times. They hung loosely around his lower calf with a Velcro strap replacing the elastic band that had lost its elasticity years earlier, holding the pant leg to his calf. On his feet, he had his old Chamonix Alpine Ascent leather hiking boots, in lieu of the more modern carbon fiber free-forming hiking and climbing boots sold in town. He had removed the wooden instep from the inner sole that gave the boot its rigidity and support for climbing some time ago, to modify the boots for hiking. He had applied multiple layers of waterproofing wax to the boot, and especially the uppers over the years that had changed the dark, tawny natural leather color of the boot to more of a honeycomb color that caused the boot to have a two-toned quality. His favorite red rip-stock nylon gaiters had been pulled down around the boot with the single stainless-steel clasp at the toe of each gaiter secured to the bottom lace, and an old piece of three millimeter purloin rope tied to the eyelet on either side of each gaiter and passed underneath his boot to secure it. Grandfather's outfit would not have been complete without his prized French carabineer that he claimed had come from the *Via Ferratain*, Austria, clipped to his belt that attempted to hold the loose-fitting knickers at a respectable height. He had discarded his old red suspenders a few years earlier when he was told they made him look old. His old cowhide fingerless gloves hung from his wrists, secured by another Velcro strap that had replaced the original leather that had torn away in a skiing mishap on a rope tow the previous winter. Grandfather claimed that the soft brown fur on the backside of the gloves that allowed him to brush away the snow from his face, had come from a grizzly bear he and his hunting mates had killed on one of their expeditions into the Brooks Range in Alaska. However,

Grandmother quietly had mentioned that the fur had actually been purchased from a JC Penny one-cent sale and had been manufactured in Duluth, Michigan. She had added the fur strip after noticing a sketch from an old hunting guide almanac Grandfather had kept in his study. His red Eddie Bauer goose down parka that he claimed could warm to minus-thirty degrees Fahrenheit, was tied around his waist in consideration of the fact that the outside temperature was still above freezing, in spite of the heavy snowfall from the early winter storm the night before. Behind him, the boy spotted the old sled that Grandfather had created from a pair of A&T cross-country skis, with a heavy wicker frame fixed to the skis at half a dozen positions. The wicker frame had just as many layers of lacquer applied as Grandfather's modified climbing boots had wax, to render it completely waterproof. The innovative sled had served its purpose of transporting firewood from the forest over many years, and signaled his grandfather's recommendation for the agenda for the day.

The A&T cross-country skis tracked through the unbroken snow on the trail with a quiet glide as Grandfather pulled the sled behind him. He had modified an old Don Willan's climbing harness into an effective pulling harness that was attached to either side of the cross-brace at the front of the sled with two lengths of five millimeter purloin rope, secured to the webbing of the harness with a locking carabineer that he tied to both ropes with a figure-eight knot. The sled matched every step that his grandfather took, maintaining a steady and sure alignment along the center of the trail. Fully loaded, the sled could carry up to half a cord of firewood; however, in recent years while the capacity of the sled had not changed, he noticed his grandfather's capacity for towing anything close to the half cord of wood had reduced significantly.

The white outback of the forest that had been changed overnight into a snowy landscape, had a mystical quality about it, and a quiet tranquility partly due to the insulating blanket of the deep snowfall on the ground. There was no one else to share the forest with them. They were very much alone, which was his grandfather's hope and intention. Most of his classmates, who were willing to brave the colder temperatures and the snowy environment following the early winter storm the night before, would have assembled at the top of Morgan's Ridge on the outskirts of the township. Pulling their contemporary-designed metal sleds to the top of the ridge, they would race down the main road that had been transformed into what closely resembled an Olympic-style bobsled run. Later in the morning, a number of his classmates' fathers, outfitted in their Gore Tex outerwear with their Helly Hanson innerwear, and their carbon-fiber mountain boots, would have fired up their two-stroke Suzuki touring snowmobiles, to pack the snow accumulated on the road, down into a nicely manicured sledding slope. Bales of hay from one of the local construction sites that had been used for erosion control, had been relocated to the bottom of the slope, providing an effective stopping barrier for the wayward sledder. He had enjoyed the opportunity to share in the sledding activity with his classmates the winter before, after realizing that his competency for sledding was based on the quality and capacity of the sled, and not the rider. If he dared the steep grade and managed to hang on to the sled until the end of the ride, he was considered on an equal basis with his classmates who had made the same successful descent. Very quickly, however, the oil and exhaust from the snowmobiles and the track of the treads crisscrossing the snow-packed roadway, would transform the pristine slope into what appeared to be a dirty industrial environment. The population on the snow-packed roadway would also grow as the day progressed, creating dangerous obstacles of people congregating at different elevations of the run, and a continuous line of snowmobiles either side of the road transporting sledders to the top of the slope again. He was pleased that his grandfather had suggested that they retrieve some of the cedar firewood he had fallen and cut earlier in the fall, that had been left by the large old cedar log that lay alongside the ravine of the creek at the top end of the trail towards the Eastern Ridge. It was an ambitious plan, since the location of the firewood was much further up the trail than they usually hiked, and would take them closer to timberline and the possibility of encountering the rare forest animal that had braved the fury of the winter storm the night before in search of food. As was his customary practice for ensuring their safety in the event they did meet any larger animals during their journeys into the forest, his grandfather always slipped his treasured rifle onto the side of the sled for the 'just-in-case scenarios.' While his winter attire dated him back to his earlier days in the Alaskan wilderness, and his tall frame no longer filled his winter clothing as it had done before through the physical conditioning of numerous hunting expeditions, his attitude towards safety remained very contemporary. Strapped to the topside of the wicker frame with a pair of quick release bungee cords, he had secured his Winchester Model 1894 that used a one-hundred-and-eighty-grain heavy cartridge bullet, and was equipped with a Bushnell 3-9 x 40 mm high-powered scope. Grandfather's one skill that he seldom talked about but that had been revered amongst his older hunting mates, was his unprecedented marksmanship. Even with the prescription glasses that he was required to wear in his older years with the start of failing eyesight, he had never lost his keen sense of touch for dead-reckoning accuracy, and could still demolish a Diet Cola can from five hundred yards. The Winchester was a powerful weapon, and in his grandfather's hands represented a formidable deterrent against any potential predators like the Eastern Ridge timber wolf. However, the wolves had become acquainted with the deadly weapon the previous fall, when Grandfather and a few of his hunting mates had chased four of the males back towards the Eastern Ridge after they had become a little too inquisitive in their reconnoiter of the school's playing field in search of food. One of the four male wolves had been mortally wounded by the high-velocity bullet fired from his grandfather's Winchester, from over three hundred yards, and the wolf pack had quickly developed a fearful respect of the lethal capability of the rifle in the hands of its owner.

Chapter 5
A Dangerous Encounter

*"For love's strength is found in love's sacrifice, and he who
suffers most has most to give."*

It had begun to snow lightly again in the later morning
a few hours into their trek, with the temperature dropping only
a few degrees. A light breeze had begun to blow through the
forest that was cooled by the blanket of snow on the ground.
The cool breeze was an added luxury with the burden of
hiking through the deeper snow deposited on the trail, causing
both the boy and his grandfather to begin to perspire heavily.
They had come prepared, with his grandfather making sure
they were both dressed appropriately with multiple layers of
clothing that could be removed or added to adjust to any
fluctuations in the air temperature or wind chill. Grandfather
had lovingly objected to his grandmother's gentle persuasion
to carry additional food and water, including the light-weight
three-man high-altitude tent that he used to carry with him
during his winter's hunting expeditions into the Alaskan
wilderness. During one of their sorties into the forest last
winter, his grandfather had suggested that they erect the tent
in the early evening with dusk beginning to cloak the forest,
and that they hike out the remaining distance the next
morning. Unbeknown to the boy, they had hiked out to within
half a kilometer of the school's maintenance buildings;
however, the overnight bivouac inside the spacious geodesic
dome tent had been the highlight of his Christmas holidays.
He had read numerous times the manufactures' marketing
description of the tent on the backside of the logo attached to
the zippered entrance canopy – *"Often copied but never*

duplicated, the VE–25 is one of the first expedition tents designed with spacious geodesic dome architecture. While the tent materials have improved over the twenty years since its introduction, the VE–25's 'keeps-you-dry design' and durability have ensured its continued popularity. The VE–25 features fully continuous pole sleeves for structural integrity, a multiple guy point design for additional stability and is capable of withstanding extreme weather, making it ideal for expeditions and high basecamps. A seventeen sq. ft. vestibule keeps Old Man Winter howling outside, and gives you room to stow boots and wet gear while you and two buddies stay dry in the tent's forty-eight sq. ft. floor area. Add internally adjustable top vents with mesh screens (so spindrift melts at the fly sheet, not on you and your gear), durable polyurethane windows, reflective guy line loops, glow-in-the-dark zipper pulls, a fly-only pitching option for summer, and you've got a versatile three-man tent designed to stand up to the worst the weather can throw at you."

The boy had learned to smile at his grandfather's overzealous commitment to being well prepared, even in the forest behind the township that rose to the base of the mountains above the Eastern Ridge and Western Escarpment. In addition to the tent, his grandmother had prepared and packed enough extra food and water to allow them to remain in the forest up to a week. As he took the point position at the beginning of their hike, he could hear his grandfather cursing under his breath about the additional weight he had been forced to carry at his grandmother's loving persuasion. But after forty-five minutes on the trail, his angst had turned to loving acceptance, as he remembered the times his grandmother's persuasion to carry additional supplies or consider alternative routes, had proven their worth on more than one occasion. At least, this was his interpretation of his grandfather's improved attitude. He also considered that his grandfather's newly acquired freedom to smoke his cherished, long thick cigars without the consternation of his grandmother, may have contributed to his cheerful disposition as well. The boy was always amazed how his grandfather could carry on a monolog conversation with him, pulling the sled up the trail through the snow and at the same time puffing on his thick cigar like a locomotive chugging up a mountainside, while he quietly labored to find each breath with each burdened step through the deep snow. It was always apparent that his grandfather was in his element in the forest and mountains, as a renewed sense of vitality seemed to give strength to his frame and step.

The cool breeze began to take on a musical quality, and occasionally the boy would march ahead of his grandfather towards a section of trail where the Douglas Fir and cedar stood tall and breast to breast, and closing his eyes, he would listen to the music of the wind blowing through the branches of the trees. He never tired of the magical orchestration of wind and trees, and the sense of peace this created in his mind. He remained standing with his eyes closed for the longest time, until he began to smell the faint hint of his grandfather's cigar smoke as he drew near. The cigar smoke had taken on a peculiar odor as though it should have been extinguished sometime earlier along the trail. He certainly was not going to make the mistake of commenting on his grandfather's cigar smoking, as his grandmother and everyone else were inclined to do. This was his environment, and he had developed a respect and admiration for his grandfather, and the way the forest and mountains had become a part of his character.

Opening his eyes, he was surprised to see that the long, thick cigar that his grandfather had been chewing on, out of the right side of his mouth while smoking at the same time, was absent from his mouth, and that his grandfather had released the bungee cords that secured the Winchester on the top frame of the sled, and was cradling the high-powered weapon in his arms. His grandfather's countenance had changed as well to reflect quite a different impression from what he was accustomed to seeing during their forest hikes. There was a look of heightened alert in his face as his chest rose and fell with quiet deliberate breathing. The boy sensed a fear rising up in his body but was unsure of what to attribute this to. His grandfather silently motioned for him to fall in behind him, and raising his forefinger to his lips, signaled him to remain quiet. His grandfather had carefully allowed the boy to hold the weapon on a few occasions, and peer through the high-powered Bushnell telescope fit to the top of the rifle. His grandfather had taught him enough about his Winchester that he knew Grandfather had already chambered a number of rounds to prepare the weapon for use. However, he was still unsure of any intended target.

He could see the big cedar tree about fifty yards up and off to the left of the trail that had remained in its original position after being struck by lightning and falling on the downhill side of the ravine years earlier. The core of the massive cedar had rotted out and had become home to a multitude of insects and small rodents and other forest animals that sought protection inside the hollowed-out tree. It had continued to decompose over the years, turning the surrounding ground into a deep brownish red coloration, as the heart of the tree was broken down by the elements over time and absorbed by the surrounding soil. The early winter storm had left a dusting of snow on top of the tree with it, protected from the heavier snowfall by the low overhanging branches of the cedars standing above. The surrounding area had been transformed into a white snowy landscape from the storm. To his untrained eye, the snowy landscape remained pristine and quiet, but his grandfather's perspective was obviously very different.

His grandfather had raised the Winchester to a shooting position, with the butt of the rifle firmly implanted against his shoulder to absorb the recoil from the blast. His right eye peered through the telescope at some distant image on the trail high above the ravine. He followed the line of the rifle with his eyes, trying to detect what had captured his grandfather's attention, but with frustration, failed to identify anything out of the ordinary. And then, as if someone had removed the slightest of veils, he noticed an ever-so-slight movement against the backdrop of the cedar tree limbs that hung low over the trail, with the weight of the snow from last night's storm. It was both the slight movement and the contrast in color between the snow-shrouded tree branches, and the darker gray of an animal that finally caught his attention. In an instant, his sense became sight as he found that he was peering back at four large and heavily muscled timber wolves that were carefully peering at the two of them.

His grandfather trained the Winchester on the four wolves as they remained stationary on the upper trail above the ravine, as he scrutinized their movements through the powerful Bushnell telescope. Even from fifty to sixty yards away without the use of the telescope, the boy began to focus on the fearless stare of the wolves. The boredom of Mrs. Imus' geography class began to take on a renewed attraction, as he considered the potential outcome of their present circumstances. While he never possessed the athleticism of many of his classmates, he had always prided himself with being a fast runner, usually as a means of retreating from an upper-grade kid who had singled him out to practice an initiation ritual in preparation for the start of the next school term. He remembered reading that the timber wolf was capable of running at speeds up to thirty to forty mph in short bursts, and while he had never actually measured his speed, he was quite confident that fueled by the rising fear he was feeling and the adrenalin pumping into his legs, he would be quite capable of giving the wolves a run for their money. Thankfully, his grandfather appeared to have the situation under control, as he raised the Winchester to a firing position, and taking careful aim just above the heads of the four large male wolves, fired off four rounds in quick succession. The four .30 to .30 cartridges traveling in excess of two thousand four hundred feet per second, found their marks in the overhanging tree limbs just above the wolves' heads, detonating a deafening explosion of splintered timber. The wolves were left unscathed, but the blasts from exploding timber had accomplished their objective, as the wolves accelerated to their top-end speed and quickly dashed up the trail towards the Eastern Ridge over a kilometer away. His grandfather continued to train the rifle on the last known position of the wolves, as he carefully scanned the immediate vicinity through the telescope. The boy felt a weakening in his legs as his body began to slightly tremble from the fear and the anxiety of the confrontation with the wolves. He turned to his grandfather to inquire about the wolves and whether or not he thought they might be back with reinforcements, and his grandfather, pivoting to face him without changing his shooting posture, raised his forefinger to his lips again, signaling him to remain quiet. His grandfather held his pose steadily as he scanned the upper trail area where they had sighted the wolves. Without flinching, his grandfather slowly lowered the aim of the Winchester, training it on a small snowy patch at the base of the large cedar tree lying in the ravine on the downhill side of the creek. The boy had sensed very quickly that the danger had not passed, and forced himself to breathe in slow, deep breaths while he tried to remain as quiet as possible. His grandfather had been able to observe the slow, labored breathing of an injured animal lying on the snowy patch of grass just behind the cedar tree. He had also been able to see with the aid of the magnification of the Bushnell telescope, the pool of blood surrounding the animal and the multiple wounds that the animal had sustained, in what appeared to be a fight to the death with the timber wolves.

There was a very noticeable and extremely unpleasant odor born on the cool breeze, very much like that of the skunk that they had encountered the previous spring. But he had learned from his grandfather that while skunks do not officially hibernate; they do become very slow or dormant during the coldest parts of winter, and are inclined to remain in the den during winter storms and heavy snowfalls. The boy remembered from his grandfather's teaching that skunks are very social animals and interact in play with one another, and apart from being able to create a stinky mess, they were not predators, and for the most part, are regarded in the same way as cats. He quickly realized that it was not a skunk that had kept his grandfather's attention on the cedar tree above and his Winchester at the ready.

His grandfather had quickly identified the dying animal as a young wolverine, and judging by his size, was still only a young adult, not fully grown. He had realized that the young wolverine had sustained mortal injuries, and it was just a matter of time before he succumbed to his extensive wounds.

Slinging the Winchester over his right shoulder, his grandfather clipped the locking carabineer attached to the purloin pull lines from the sled back onto the Willan's climbing harness, and began to slowly advance with sled in tow towards the fallen cedar and the site of the dying animal. The boy quietly fell in line behind the sled as his grandfather quickly glanced at him and gave him a quick grin and a nod of affirmation, and then turned his attention back towards the trail in front of him. It was apparent by his grandfather's body language that the imminent danger from the wolves had passed. As he neared closer to the dying animal, his grandfather quickly grasped the rifle from his shoulder, keeping it at the ready with both hands, grasping the stalk of the weapon with it deliberately pointing down towards the trail floor.

It was only a matter of minutes before they were within view of the wounded wolverine. The boy could hardly contain himself with feelings of excitement and fear that were racing through his mind and body. The animal did not appear quite as ferocious as its reputation and legends had suggested; resembling the size of a large dog with thick, dark, and oily fur that had been heavily matted with blood and filled with timber splinters and debris from the undergrowth of the forest. Even in the wolverine's quiet resting position, he appeared stocky with muscular short legs, and a broad and rounded head. His legs were covered with deep bite wounds from the wolves' repeated attacks, and the dried blood on the front and back of his neck were telltale signs that the wolves had inflicted numerous seemingly fatal bites. And yet the young wolverine lived on, although that appeared to be only for a short time before the wolves returned to finish him off, or his remaining energy and resolve to survive succumbed to the harsh elements.

His grandfather slowly unclipped the carabineer from his climbing harness and left the sled in the center of the trail adjacent to the fallen cedar and the resting place of the wolverine. His serious facial expression and his outstretched arm with his forefinger extended, pointing towards the front of the sled, was a clear signal for the boy to remain with the sled as his grandfather carefully approached the wounded animal. The Winchester remained trained on the wolverine's still body, with only a very slight rise and fall of the animal's chest from almost undetectable silent breaths. His grandfather had a reputation as an accomplished Alaskan hunting guide and avid outdoor man. He was often approached by journalists from the local newspaper or occasionally from larger publications such as *Field and Stream* and *North American Hunter,* to give an account of one of his numerous hunting expeditions into the Alaskan interior, or to review a new product line scheduled to be launched to the hunting community. What many people didn't know was that Grandfather was also an avid conservationist, and supporter of numerous wildlife organizations that protected animals and their habitats. The years of hunting bear, moose, deer, elk and caribou in the untamed Alaskan wilderness, and the time he had spent in areas such as the Brooks Range, circumnavigating Denali National Park, and popular hunting areas in the Yukon, had instilled in him a deep love and respect for the environment, and compassion for the wildlife that made this untamed outback their home.

Nevertheless, it was still a surprise to the boy when his grandfather motioned for him to bring the sled up the trail and into the ravine to where he was squatted down next to the wolverine on the backside of the fallen cedar. As the boy stepped into the small snowy clearing with sled in tow, he was startled by the small eyes of the wolverine looking out at him with an unusual intelligence and hopefulness. He had expected to see the lifeless expression of an animal near death as he had seen on other occasions during their excursions into the forest. He also noticed that the short-rounded ears of the animal were cocked in a position of alertness, as he carefully observed his grandfather's slightest movement. As the boy approached the wolverine closer, he noticed that the young animal's body was trembling involuntarily, perhaps from the significant loss of blood from the near fatal attack by the wolves, and also from his fear of the encounter with the humans. His grandfather pointed out to the boy that the animal's vertebrae had been partially severed from the vicious bite to his neck by one of the larger male wolves, but amazingly had not proved to be fatal. It had, however, rendered the young wolverine temporarily paralyzed, which still didn't diminish the boy's concern as he stooped down and looked into the face of the wolverine, as their eyes met in a long sympathetic stare.

The boy noticed that close up to the animal, the pungent odor from the wolverine was masked by the light snowfall from earlier in the day that had dusted over the top of his body. His grandfather had brushed away the snow from his body with the bear fur lining on the backside of his glove, to reveal multiple bite wounds that had penetrated his skin with the blood dried from the cooling temperatures as the day progressed into the later afternoon. The extent of the animal's injuries drew out a deep compassionate expression on his grandfather's face. The boy was amazed at the determination of the young animal to have survived against all odds, and began to feel his own sense of compassion well up inside him as he stared at the motionless body of the animal. The legends and rare stories of encounters with this fearsome creature that the boy had become all too familiar with, passed into obscurity as he observed the helplessness of a once-fearsome predator, lying and trembling before him. His heart felt a strong compassion for the young wolverine as he looked across at the moistened eyes of his grandfather, as he brushed back a tear that slowly trickled down his cheek with the backside of his glove. It became immediately apparent that his grandfather had no intention of disposing of the young animal with his Winchester, or leaving him to the hungry wolves that certainly would be circling back in the next few hours to make their final kill. His grandfather had taken one of the water bottles from the pack secured to the sled, and was slowly dripping a trickle of water into the animal's mouth and on to his tongue that the animal had almost purposely extended to find the refreshing moisture. A thousand different thoughts began to fill his head, as he considered the possible consequences of what his grandfather was suggesting with his actions.

The young wolverine lay perfectly still as Grandfather gently rubbed snow across the bite wounds on his body and legs, absorbing the dried blood and providing an instant analgesic with the coldness from the snow that began to deaden the pain the wolverine was obviously feeling. His grandfather easily elevated the young animal as he motioned for the boy to slide the rainfly from the tent, that his grandfather had removed from the VE-24 tent bag, underneath the wolverine. The animal continued to lie motionless in his grandfather's arms, partly because of the paralysis from the wounds he had sustained, and also because of a growing recognition that the hunter and the boy appeared to mean him no harm. His grandfather cut a number of smaller cedar branches with his ten-inch-long Kershaw-fixed blade hunting knife that he always kept in the front pocket of his pack. He removed the fresh dusting of snow from each branch as he laid the individual branches onto the sled, creating a makeshift bedding to soften the rigid wicker base of the sled. Once the animal was centered on the rainfly, his grandfather gently pulled him up onto the cedar bedding in the center of the sled, and laid the main tent section over the top of the wolverine for warmth. His grandfather removed a coiled section of five millimeter purloin climbing rope from his pack, and began to secure the injured animal to the wicker frame with the tent fly neatly draped over the top of him. The boy helped to tether the tent fabric as his grandfather tied the rope with a half-hitch to each section of the side rails. The young wolverine continued to lie motionless atop the cedar bedding on the center of the sled, as the hunter and the boy gently secured him to the wicker frame. The boy noticed in his grandfather's eyes that the casual expression that was often illuminated in his face during their hikes into the forest for firewood, had been replaced with a determination and alertness he had never seen before, as his grandfather readied the sled and its patient for transport down the trail. He also noticed that his grandfather had not secured the Winchester back onto the side of the sled with the bungee cords, but instead slung the rifle over his right shoulder with the shoulder sling holding the weapon tightly against his back. The boy helped his grandfather turn the sled to face the downward section of the trail, with its patient neatly secured. With his arm outstretched a second time and his forefinger extended, his grandfather silently pointed to a few yards in front of the locking carabineer that he had dropped in the snow, still attached to the purloin pull lines from the sled, signaling the boy to take up the point position but within arm's reach of his grandfather. In the next instant, his grandfather had clipped the locking carabineer onto the webbing at the back of the climbing harness, re-sheathed his Kershaw hunting knife in its leather sheath attached to his belt at his left side, and slowly took up the slack in the pull ropes, as he began effortlessly moving forward down the trail. Little did the boy realize at the time how his entire life would be altered from their unusual discovery of the young wolverine, and their compassionate intervention for the welfare of the seriously injured animal. The boy also realized that they were not out of the woods yet, so to speak, and there was still the imminent danger from the returning wolves that both he and his grandfather were quietly aware of as they began their descent down the trail.

Chapter 6
The Pinnacle

*"Heroes are forged on anvils hot with pain, and splendid
courage comes but with the test;
Some natures ripen and some natures bloom only on blood-
wet soil; some souls prove great only in moment's dark with
death or doom.
But you will not mind the roughness, nor the steepness of the
way; nor the cold, unrested morning, nor the heat of the
noonday;
And you will not take a turning to the left or the right but go
straight ahead, nor tremble at the coming of the night, for
the road leads home."*

The boy and his grandfather had advanced only a few meters
down the trail with the sled and young wolverine in tow when
they began to sense the impending presence of the timber
wolves staring viciously from their concealment behind the
stand of cedars close by, searching for a tactical opportunity

to attack and overcome their intended prey. Perhaps for the first time in his life, the boy began to be aware of his mortality, although it was in fleeting glances as fear and panic cloaked any sense of reason. A dense fog began to slowly creep up through the forest from the valley below, as the air temperature cooled and visibility began to diminish. Although the temperature had dropped noticeably as dusk began to set in, the boy observed beads of perspiration forming on his grandfather's forehead and brow. He realized that this was not a result of any physical exertion, since they had remained stationary for the last five minutes scrutinizing the surrounding forest that seemed to have come alive with movement. His grandfather motioned for the boy to assume a point position a few meters in front of the sled. The boy took a few shallow gasps of breath, questioning his grandfather's wisdom of placing him in harm's way of the wolves, as he obediently took up his position. A few breaths later, he realized his grandfather's loving protection in his instruction.

The summer before, they had bivouacked on the Pinnacle after an exhausting day of reconnoitering the forest for fallen timber. A particularly brutal summer storm had lashed the region the week before, leaving entire firs and cedars upturned in its maelstrom. The Pinnacle was a massive granite geological formation that resembled an upside-down spire with a near shear vertical face and a small, flat cleared area about thirty square meters on the very top. Access to the top of the Pinnacle was by way of a goat track about two hundred meters off the main trail that joined the last switchback before the final descent. The track was just wide enough to allow single file movement with no turnouts until you either reached the small clearing on top, or retraced your steps back to the main trail. The convergence of the Pinnacle's goat track and the main trail was a logistic milestone representing approximately three-fourths of a kilometer to the trail head below via a series of switchbacks. Views of sunrise or sunset from the top of the Pinnacle were not for the fainthearted. The vertical drop to the valley below created awe and trepidation in even the most experienced mountaineers who attempted to navigate imaginary routes up the sheer rock face with little more than the slightest of thumb depressions in the face for leverage. Their bivouac had been particularly memorable with three of Grandfather's friends joining them in the late afternoon. The boy listened with fascination as his grandfather and his hunting mates shared their stories and adventures of hunting and mountaineering in the Alaskan wilderness. Grandfather's close friend Dewey, had recounted a particular incident involving a pack of Alaskan timber wolves who had been stalking the same black bear they had been tracking for three days. He described with vivid realism the cunning hunting tactics of the timber wolf. While the timber wolves never backed down from a fight, their preemptive strategy in pursuing prey was typically from a position of stealth, and a rear or flanked assault. The knowledge he had gleaned from Dewey's story the summer before did little to repress his present fear. It did, however, give affectionate meaning to his grandfather's gesture.

It had begun to snow again lightly, which aggravated the conditions for them against the timber wolves. His grandfather quietly scanned the forest in the back of them and to each side, and then quickly, unslinging the Winchester from across his right shoulder, he aimed skyward and fired off three rapid bursts of the powerful one-hundred-and-eighty-grain cartridges. The shroud of fog, darkness, and snow, unsuccessfully attempted to stifle the thunderous sound of the Winchester as the bullets were jettisoned somewhere into the stratosphere. Lowering the rifle slightly but still at the ready, he listened intently for any response to his shots or movement in the surrounding forest. A few moments later, with a strange look of satisfaction on his face, he re-slung the Winchester over his right shoulder, and with the slightest nod of his head, beckoned the boy to begin moving down the trail as he followed with the sled and the young wolverine tethered to the wicker frame.

The weather conditions quickly deteriorated, as a strong cold wind began to blow down from the ridges above, and the falling snow picked up intensity with the wind as it began to create stinging sensations, blowing horizontally against his face. His grandfather, however, didn't reveal the slightest sense of discomfort as he marked pace with the sled in tow to what appeared to be their next logical stopping point where the trail switched back on itself at the junction with the goat track that led to the Pinnacle. The boy shot a quick glance towards the wolverine who remained motionless under the rainfly on top of the sled.

They covered the seventy meters to the switchback in about fifteen minutes. The boy realized he was trembling from a combination of fear and the cold that had begun to chill him to the bone. His grandfather quickly evaluated their physical needs, and skillfully maneuvered the sled so it was straddling the trail immediately above the switchback, creating a temporary barrier, with the young wolverine appearing to be offered as a sacrifice to the ravenous wolves. The weather had deteriorated even further to the point where his grandfather had become a ghostly silhouette, although he stood only a few meters from the boy. His grandfather carefully searched what had rapidly become a frozen snow-enshrouded landscape, for the slightest sense of movement from their predators. A few moments later, his grandfather motioned for the boy to begin moving off along the goat track that led to the Pinnacle two hundred meters to the end of the narrow trail. The boy dutifully, but with certain trepidation, took a half dozen steps down the trail into the eerie thick fog. A moment later, he was struck with fear as he heard what appeared to be a heavy thump that produced a small tremor on the trail that drained his legs of any remaining strength. Reeling around quickly, he made out the shadow of his grandfather standing in front of the sled and realized how he must have singlehandedly lifted the sled with the wolverine onto the goat track, so that the sled was aligned with the trail heading towards the Pinnacle. The boy could hear his grandfather strap the pull harness to himself and clipping the carabineers into position to begin towing the sled down the goat track towards the Pinnacle. The boy remained motionless as he waited for his grandfather to come to his position with sled in tow, so the two of them could proceed along the goat track together.

The snow had quickly drifted up to about twenty centimeters on the goat track with the storm continuing to intensify. The outline of the track had become concealed by the snowdrift, and appeared as part of the slope falling away to the steepness of the grade and an eventual plummet to the valley floor about four hundred meters below. The boy had remembered the summer before, how his grandfather had tethered him with the five-millimeter purloin climbing rope attached to a modified climbing harness to prevent an accidental fall and maintain a sense of confidence for the boy, as he traversed the narrow track towards the Pinnacle. The boy also remembered the ideal conditions with a light, cool breeze of summer whispering through the firs and cedars, and the dry, even footing along the goat track during that memorable summer trek. Even in perfect conditions, the goat track still struck fear into his spirit as he imagined the consequences of an unchecked fall amidst his grandfather's encouraging words not to look down. Turning to face his grandfather in search of encouraging words, he looked into his face, and for the first time during the last twenty-four hours, he recognized the weariness and fatigue etched on his face from the stress of the deadly pursuit that was weakening his resources.

His grandfather had attempted on numerous occasions to teach the boy not to judge any situation with the question of 'what should I do now,' but instead, formulate a plan in response to the situation, based on the facts and resources available. Up until this moment, this challenge always seemed to represent one of those very deep spiritual truths that his grandfather tried unsuccessfully to instill in the boy's spirit, but for the first time in his life, recognizing his grandfather's failing strength, the boy began to consider the truth of this notion. The boy had become aware of how akin their spirits were to each other, although they were separated by over fifty years of age. He had recognized that their relationship had experienced a deep bonding through sharing in the roughness and steepness of the way, and in the moment's dark with death and possible doom. Imagining the safety of the climbing harness tethered to the climbing rope held in his grandfather's hands, the boy turned about and faced the goat track as he began to cautiously traverse the trail towards the Pinnacle beyond.

The temperature had fallen well below zero, causing the snow to be as light as feathers. His grandfather had shared accounts of the rare artic storm that swept down from the frigid north, changing the forest into a frozen landscape, accompanied with mighty winds, heavy snowfalls, and subarctic conditions. The boy's fascination in these stories was rapidly becoming a reality, as he moved slowly through the drifted snow. He easily kicked the light, dry snow forward out of his way with each step, but suffered the agony of the snow being caught by the blowing wind, piercing his unprotected face with sharp ice-like slivers that seemed to penetrate even his multiple layers of clothing. The boy knew that his grandfather's mind was to reach the small clearing atop the Pinnacle as quickly as possible, erect the VE-25, and tether it securely to the surrounding rock-outcroppings and retreat inside, taking shelter from the intensifying storm and pursuit of their predators.

Every ten to fifteen minutes, the boy turned and faced his grandfather with a look of strong resolve as his only means of encouraging him in his strenuous task of towing the sled with the wolverine secured on top the wicker basket. He helped his grandfather remove the snow buildup in front of the sled, and resuming his lead position about two meters in front of his grandfather, continued cutting a path through the deepening snowdrift. The storm was unrelenting, and the rapid transition from the dark gray of the storm to the darkness of the night, partially shrouded their arrival to the small clearing on top of the Pinnacle. Without need for conversation or instruction, the boy and his grandfather fell in line with their respective duties in erecting the VE-25. The boy quickly removed the steel tent pegs, purloin guy lines, and climbing hammer from the rip-stock nylon storage bag, and placed one set at each of the four corners of the VE-25 that his grandfather had stretched out over the small clearing. Working from corner to corner, his grandfather secured one corner and then pulled taut the adjoining corner until it met with a satisfying 'twang.' The boy had already retrieved the telescoping support poles, and had stitched them through the eyelets attached to the ribs of the tent as he had rehearsed on numerous occasions before. The tent was quickly erected, and his grandfather finished tightening the final purloin guy lines to the steel tent pegs as the boy began removing the supplies from the sled and transporting them into the tent. His grandfather made his first appearance inside the tent, and quickly arranged a cleared section along one side of the tent for the injured wolverine. With renewed strength and speed to meet the occasion, his grandfather lovingly and gently laid the wolverine on top of the canvas tent bag that he had arranged into a comfortable bed. The duck-down sleeping bags were quickly rolled out on top of the Styrofoam mattresses, and the boy dove into the warmth and security of his bag as his grandfather carefully laid his Winchester rifle to his right side, between himself and the Wolverine, with an opened box of one-hundred-and-fifty-grain cartridges at the ready. Grandfather glanced at the boy with a faint smile that seemed to contain richness of encouragement, pride, and conversation, but without audible words, as they both lay quietly inside their sleeping bags, waiting for the storm to pass, or their final confrontation with the timber wolves.

The VE-25 was living up to its promotional propaganda in providing unforeseen comfort and security inside the tent from the intensifying storm outside. Exhaustion had silenced both the boy and his grandfather to wordless recognition of each other's presence. The boy glanced at the injured wolverine lying ever so still in the cleared section atop the makeshift bed his grandfather had fashioned out of the canvas tent bag. He had created a small semicircular partition around one side of the wolverine's bed that faced into the interior of the tent from supplies retrieved from the sled. The small separation wall was his grandfather's attempt to alleviate any further stress the wolverine might experience with being in close proximity to humans. The boy could see the faint rise and fall of the wolverine's chest and side over the top of the small wall, and began to wonder what kind of resolve the animal must have to live in spite of the mortal injuries inflicted by the timber wolves. As the air inside the tent began to warm from their body heat, the boy also began to smell the unpleasant scent of the wolverine's wet fur mixed with dried blood. The inactivity of lying down after so much physical exertion, and the warmth generated from his body heat inside the sleeping bag, began to have a tranquilizing effect on the boy's senses as his eyes closed and he lay motionless in an exhausted stupor. Time seemed to stand still in the heaviness of his sleep as he was woken a short time later by the hand of his grandfather laid gently over his mouth. Looking up into his grandfather's face, he noticed that his eyes revealed a sense of cunningness and shrewdness, while his open lips exposed a silent "shhhhh," warning the boy to continue quietness in speech and action. The boy noticed that the inside fabric walls of the tent had become still where they had previously rippled violently from the raging storm outside. The storm had passed and left an eerie silence over the forest that had been transformed into an arctic landscape. The boy focused all his attention on identifying any recognizable sounds from outside the tent. And then in the disturbing silence, he heard the faint, deep growl of the timber wolf, perhaps somewhere close to the head of the goat track that veered off the main trail towards the Pinnacle.

Chapter 7
Against All Hope

"Let hope be not quenched in the blackness of night, though the cyclone awhile may have blotted the light; for behind the great darkness the stars ever shine, and the light of God's heaven, His love will make thine."

The atmosphere seemed to be enshrouded in an air of anticipation of some impending tragedy, as the boy considered the audible telltale signs of the timber wolves from inside the presumed security of the VE-24. His grandfather quietly moved to a position in front of the main entry fly and began to slowly unzip the fabric of the double-walled geodetic tent to expose the entry vestibule. The storm had deposited up to six hundred millimeters of snow throughout the night that had drifted into a natural wall just outside the vestibule, partially obscuring the entry from anyone or anything intent in gaining access inside the tent. His grandfather silently guided the zippers to the bottom of their tracks and gently rolled the entry fly, securing it with the tied cord on either side, allowing the softness of the morning light to illuminate the inside of the tent, and for the first time exposing the face of the injured wolverine. The boy gazed into the eyes of the wolverine and was surprised to see what appeared to be a passion and determination to live, blotting out any fear of the savagery of the timber wolves that the boy expected to detect. In a fleeting moment, he felt a growing nervousness with his close proximity to what he had been led to believe was a ferocious carnivore and predator, as the wolverine lay wounded atop the canvas tent bag.

Grandfather handed him one of the screw-cap wide-mouth stainless steel water bottles from the side pocket of his backpack that lay next to the wolverine, and with a wordless impression of concern, motioned with his head and eyes towards the injured animal. The boy quickly perceived his grandfather's suggestion of giving water to rehydrate the wolverine's wounded body from the loss of blood following the attack by the timber wolves, and administer first aid that had earlier been overshadowed by the stressful descent to the Pinnacle that took precedence over providing practical aid to the injured animal. He stared at the water bottle in his right hand as his grandfather retrieved the Winchester and with stealth, began to quietly exit the tent through the vestibule. The boy attempted to convince himself to believe that the wolverine was completely incapacitated as a result of his injuries sustained during the attack, and that any sudden defensive movement was impractical. Nevertheless, his hand holding the water bottle remained petrified by his fear of the impossible becoming a reality inside the tent with his grandfather now out of reach to provide needed support. The boy was startled by the sudden slow movement of the wolverine opening his mouth, and exposing a row of long incisors in the pink flesh of his mouth as he painfully extended his tongue. A subtle smile registered on his face as he observed the wolverine perceiving the situation between the two of them, and willed his hand to tilt the water bottle to dispense a few priceless water droplets onto the surface of the wolverine's tongue. The injured animal painfully rolled its tongue to the back of its mouth to moisten the pink flesh that appeared dry and tainted with blood, and equally painfully attempted to swallow the few droplets of water that remained on its tongue. As the boy continued to dispense the water, the wolverine began to move slightly to adjust its position atop the canvas tent bag, as it appeared to experience some degree of refreshment, although it was barely visible apart from the deeper breathing contractions that registered in more rhythmic rising and falling of its chest, compared to the shallow contractions that the boy and his grandfather noticed when they first tethered the injured animal to the top of the sled.

As the wolverine began to quietly lap the water, the boy sensed a strange feeling of compassion as tears dampened his eyes. He comprehended that the wolverine had survived horrific injuries at the jaws of the timber wolves, and what must have been immeasurable despair as he witnessed his pack slaughtered by the wolves. He began to consider what kind of feelings an animal such as this felt over profound loss. Did it resemble similar feelings that humans experienced? With apprehension, the boy bravely reached out his hand and softly rested it on the wolverine's head, with only the slightest stir of recognition by the wolverine.

The boy repeated the action of dispensing small droplets of water onto the wolverine's tongue, but with diminishing trepidation as he began to experience a surreal feeling of calm and peace in such close proximity to the wounded animal that seemed to momentarily quell the sense of impending danger, he and his grandfather had been subjected to the whole of the last day.

Chapter 8
Helpless Surroundings

"A long, long road I traveled night and day and sought to find within myself some way. Nothing I did or felt could bring me near. Self-effort failed, and I was filled with fear."

The boy's feelings of tranquility were quickly replaced with a cold chill of fear at the faint sound of the low, deep growl of a timber wolf directly outside the tent, separated only by the paper-thin rip-stock nylon wall of the VE 25. In the same instant, the wolverine's eyes came to life growing larger, with the fur on the back of its neck standing erect at the sound of the faint breathing of the wolf, separated only by sight.

The quietness of the morning and stillness of the forest behind the Pinnacle, suddenly exploded with the thunderous boom from Grandfather's Winchester Model 1894 hunting rifle. It was only an instant from when the boy recognized the sound of his grandfather chambering the one-hundred-and-eighty-grain bullet, until he saw the reddish glow of the muzzle flash through the tent fabric, and smelled the burnt gunpowder that was less than half a breath away. The dull thud of the bullet penetrating flesh was instantaneous, with the bullet traveling at a velocity of almost two thousand-five hundred feet per second.

The blast from his grandfather's Winchester rifle was deafening, as it thundered throughout the forest to the Eastern Ridge; however, the penetration of the bullet through the flesh and heart of the timber wolf registered barely an audible 'zip' with precision accuracy, delivering a mortal wound to the attacking wolf, dropping it instantly dead in its tracks. The blood splatter on the outside of the nylon wall of the VE-25 immediately caused a feeling of revulsion mixed with relief, as the boy realized that his grandfather had once again demonstrated his unfailing love and protection.

The boy leaped to his feet and in the same motion flew through the tent vestibule, landing a few meters behind his grandfather. He quickly weighed the situation, counting five large timber wolves, preparing to attack with no more than ten meters separating the predators from the tent. A sixth wolf lay motionless about three meters from his grandfather, with a huge hole in the right side of what used to be its head and jaw. Out of the corner of his eye, the boy was alerted to the movement of another large wolf moving stealthily to the rear of the tent. His grandfather quickly chambered another bullet as he swung his body to the right with death reckoning on the wolf that had disappeared behind the rear of the tent. A second deafening explosion erupted from the Winchester behind the opposite side of the tent, with the surrounding snow splattered in blood and the boy's ears ringing from the blast.

His grandfather had reduced the pursuers by three; however, the boy quickly recognized the futility of their circumstances, with an attack by the remaining wolves imminent.

Without turning his back on the wolves and yet not attempting to stare them down and creating a threat, his grandfather motioned for the boy to slowly retreat into the enclosure of the tent, while he bravely stood his ground over the protection of the boy and the injured wolverine. The attackers appeared to be seriously considering the condition of their three fallen companions, and any further advancement with the cool of the morning fouled with the smell of blood and gunpowder from the lethal work of the Winchester. As the boy's sight adjusted to the change in light inside the tent, he noticed the wolverine's eyes had become very large, reflecting stressfulness apparently from the sound of the attacking wolves and gunshot blasts. The boy once again gently rested his hand on the head of the wolverine, offering some degree of comfort as he noticed its body trembling from fear following the confrontation with the timber wolves. The boy also began to recognize the slightest sensation of unyielding strength building deep inside him, in determining to prevail in his hopeless surroundings.

The boy could hear the deep and bottomless growl from the wolves, signifying that they had not moved from their earlier position of being poised for a final attack. He observed his grandfather through the open tent vestibule, remaining motionless as he continued to blockade the entrance to the tent with the Winchester at the low-ready position, with the seat of the butt of the rifle firmly set in his right shoulder, ready to raise the rifle, take aim, and fire if the wolves decided to attack.

Chapter 9
Joyful Relief

"Hope finds its strength in helplessness."

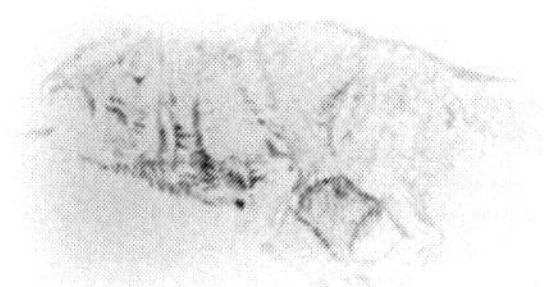

In the anxious stillness of the standoff between his grandfather and the remaining timber wolves, the boy recognized the very faint, yet distinctly audible voices of approaching men carried on the shroud of tension created by the encounter between Grandfather and the wolves, as they descended along the goat track towards the Pinnacle.

A light waft of wind created ripples on the tent wall as a prelude to the eruption of the thundering sound of Dewey's Remington Gauge Shotgun, Winston's Ruger 10/22 Rifle, and Audrey's Remington Model 700-Springfield, as Grandfather's hunting partners emptied an overabundance of cartridges into the open air above the timber wolves. As the boy emerged from the tent a second time, only the flurry of snow at the heels of the rapidly retreating wolves up the steep slope to the Eastern Ridge, chronicled their earlier marauding presence.

As Grandfather and his hunting mates gazed silently at one another following the exodus of the timber wolves, they began to weigh the surrounding telltale signs of the wolves' previous advance. The boy noticed an obvious yet quiet sigh of relief of Grandfather's appreciation of his mates' prompt response, and action to his three rapid bursts of the powerful one-hundred-and-eighty-grain cartridges fired from his Winchester earlier. The three short bursts from the hunters' powerful rifles into the open air, had become a well-known warning sign of impending danger and need of immediate support that Grandfather and his hunting mates had established during the many years of hunting in the remote areas of mainland Alaska along the upper branch of the Coleen River, in what was now the Arctic National Wildlife Refuge, close to the Canadian border, about ninety miles from the villages of Old Crow in the Yukon Territory, and Arctic Village in Alaska's Brook Range.

Without the exchange of words, Winston and Audrey were the first to break the silence of the silent gaze as they began moving the carcass of the dead wolves lying next to the outside walls of the tent, where all signs of life and power had been extinguished by Grandfather's powerful Winchester. The slaughtered wolves were positioned a stone's throw upslope from the tent, camouflaged by the dense undergrowth laden with freshly fallen snow, and the wind-drifted snow ridges that had blown into seemingly permanent monuments by the turbulent storm the night before. The birds and scavenging forest animals and insects would reduce the bodies of the wolves in a few short days until any trace of the predators was erased from the landscape.

The two hunters proceeded to clean the external walls of the tent, along with the splattered blood left from the swift execution of the attacking wolves, trampling the surrounding area with the freshly fallen snow to erase any sign of the terrible event that had transpired a short time earlier that continued to haunt the boy and his grandfather.

The boy's grandfather moved to face the entrance to the tent, opening the zippered tent vestibule that had been left partially closed following the boy's earlier hasty exit to join his grandfather at his side to face the ravenous wolves. His grandfather rolled back the two halves of the vestibule, tethering them to the fixing loops stitched to either side of the frame of the opening, to completely expose the inside of the tent to the morning light, illuminating the still silhouette of the injured wolverine lying quietly atop the canvas tent bag that Grandfather had earlier fashioned into a comfortable bed. Motioning for his hunting partners to peer into the tent, the three of them were transfixed in what they saw with the wolverine lying motionless but fully conscious with its dark brown eyes enlarged and returning its stare back at the hunters.

Instantly, Grandfather's hunting partners recognized the deeper meaning that provided a fuller understanding of the boy and his grandfather's ordeal with the wolverine, as they felt a surge of admiration and respect for their hunting partners' transition from his earlier reputation of famed hunting guide in the Alaskan wilderness, to conservationist with a commitment to the protection and preservation of the environment that had become his life's ambition.

The boy recognized the expression of fear on the wolverine's face as the injured animal peered back through the tent opening at the three hunters with weapons held in front of them at the ready, against their brightly colored hunting vests by a tactical single shoulder sling but aimed harmlessly at the ground. The boy inched past the hunters back into the tent and took up his previous position next to the wolverine. In spite of the hunters' many years tracking big game in the Alaskan wilderness, facing the extremes of the Alaskan environment and harsh climate, sharing in numerous life, and death encounters with Alaskan polar bears, angry moose, attacking wolves, and grizzly bears, they all stood astonished as they witnessed the boy's act of compassion, as he reached out and placed his right hand on the brow of the wolverine, registering an immediate conversion of fear to comfort on the expression of the injured animal. They were further speechless when the boy calmly began dropping small droplets of water from the wide-mouth stainless-steel water bottle left lying next to the wolverine, onto the anxiously waiting tongue that had once again been extended to collect the hydrating relief to the animal from the water.

The VE-28 had served its purpose well, and it was agreed amongst the hunters that the tent would be carefully dismantled around the injured wolverine to lessen any further trauma or fear to the injured animal. Once the tent was securely tethered to the wicker sled, the hunters lifted the wolverine and gently positioned him atop the tent that had been neatly folded with the collapsible tent poles secured to the side of the sled. The five-millimeter purloin climbing rope had been stitched back and forth across the folded tent, looping through the timber eyelets drilled into the top portion of the runners either side of the sled, to ensure the tent would remain immovable during the descent to the trailhead below. When Grandfather was satisfied that the wolverine appeared comfortably positioned in its bed atop the tent, the rip-stock nylon flysheet was draped over the injured animal and secured to the same timber eyelets with light gauge dynamic purloin accessory cord that resembled a crafted matrix of lattice.

Grandfather's three hunting mates made quick work, positioning the sled with its injured patient to align with the entrance to the goat track that led from the Pinnacle back to the intersection of the main trail two hundred meters back up the slope. Dewey shouldered his Remington Shotgun and tethered it to his back, and began to clip himself into the pull-harness connected to the sled and secure the locking carabiners without any protest from Grandfather. The boy took up a position directly behind the sled to afford the injured wolverine a sliver of sight with his grandfather assuming the point position and his Remington at the ready. Winston and Audrey fell in single file behind the boy, with their weapons still held at the ready in front of them by the tactical single shoulder sling against their brightly colored hunting vests.

The morning began to come alive with random beams of sunshine filtering through the branches of the Douglas fir and cedar, awakening the forest to robins, white crowned sparrows, and thrushes darting from one vantage point to another, observing the group of the boy, his grandfather, and the hunters preparing to depart the Pinnacle. The fleeting streams of sunshine warmed the needles on the branches of the trees, releasing the familiar fragrance of the forest as the boy pondered the events of the last few days from their discovery of the injured wolverine, his grandfather's decision to rescue the animal, and the terrifying encounter with the timber wolves that left the boy still feeling nervousness despite the support provided by the presence of his grandfather's hunting mates. The boy recognized that something had changed inside himself since they entered the forest a few short days ago, possibly in his spirit and soul that his grandfather often referred to with little interest reciprocated previously from the boy. Certainly, his pride and respect for his grandfather had grown and matured, as he had observed his grandfather's response to their unprecedented circumstances, with a prideful admiration registering on his flushed face in a gentle smile, as he considered his grandfather's loving protection in his unfaltering stand against the timber wolves. He also recognized something that seemed to be a confidence in himself that was quite foreign to his shallow understanding of his character, that had never been challenged by the adversity of extraordinary circumstances that had forced him to consider his own mortality. A new meaning well-lit his thoughts of his grandfather's words that he had recited numerous times in the past, of the camaraderie that he and his hunting mates had been bound together through extreme circumstances and danger. Words that his grandfather had shared with him numerous times in the past, that had fallen to the ground with little respect and consideration, now caused him to sense a pang in his soul of shame. The boy glanced at the dark eyes of the wolverine peering hopefully out from under the tethered tent fly, and felt a soft pull of compassion for the injured animal, recognizing that a silent bond had also formed between him and the injured animal through the terrifying ordeal with the wolves.

Audrey tied a length of five-millimeter purloin climbing rope to the timber eyelet in the back frame of the sled, skillfully tied a figure-eight loop at the trailing end of the rope, and clipped the loop into the locking carabiner fastened to the climbing harness he had secured around his waist, providing an effective braking mechanism for the sled during the descent to the trail head three-fourths of a kilometer below. As the group prepared to depart the Pinnacle, the boy realized that something indeed had changed in him.

Chapter 10
The Final Descent

I will know by the gleam and glitter, of the golden chain you wear,
By your heart's calm strength in loving, of the fire you have had to bear.
Beat on, true heart, forever; shine bright, strong golden chain;
And bless the cleansing fire and the furnace of living pain.

The fog and low-lying cloud that had enshrouded the forest scenery began to dissipate as the morning sun began to warm the air temperature, causing the fog to rise, revealing the wintry landscape and the effects of the fury of the winter storm the day and night before. The path of descent to the trailhead below became illuminated with the clearing of the fog and the sun shining on the unbroken snow that had built up on the trail, providing a smooth and unencumbered surface for the sled to track on. The incline of the grade that descended to the valley below was relatively steep; however, the trail had been carved out of the slope with numerous switchbacks that led up through the granite hill to reduce the grade, providing hikers run-outs that incorporated rest-stops at the junction of each switchback, as the trail turned to traverse the slope in the opposite direction, crossing muddy seeps during the spring and summer that had frozen. The route to the trailhead provided magnificent views of the valley below, and wonderful vantage points for amateur photographers to capture fiery orange sunrises that turned the color of the landscape to pink, as the sun rose above the horizon.

The route was approximately three-fourths of a kilometer from the confluence of the goat track to the trailhead, crossing Pinnacle Creek on a small rock bridge about two hundred meters before opening into the clearing at the trailhead. The boy studied the branches of the fir and cedars as the party slowly descended with the sled in tow, observing the cool gentle wind blowing down from the Eastern Ridge, releasing snowflakes from the snow-laden branches with the snow crystals capturing the beams of the morning sun, changing their appearance to seeming diamonds as the crystals evaporated into the air.

The forest was relatively quiet except for small rodents including red and gray squirrels scurrying across the trail and throughout the dense landscape in search of food. The boy had to check his imagination for timber wolves hiding within the dense undergrowth. Grandfather had taken point-position in front of Dewey, pulling the sled as the party descended the first switchback on the route to the trailhead below. All of a sudden Grandfather held up his hand, demanding silence that brought the rescue party to a stop. The faintest of sounds had caught his attention, and he strained to hear and identify the sound. There it was again, a rustling that differed from the wind in the trees. Grandfather and his hunting mates raised their weapons in readiness, anticipating the possibility of a second stealth attack by the timber wolves.

Cautiously, a Black-tailed deer with its young fawn emerged from the dense undergrowth and timidly crossed the trail about ten meters in front of the rescue party, quickly disappearing into the thick bush on the opposite side, much to the relief of the boy, his grandfather, and his hunting mates. Nevertheless, the encounter with the deer and its fawn rather than the timber wolves did little to disperse the boy's feelings of nervousness.

As the rescue party approached the end of the first switchback, the boy spied a small party of early-morning hikers waiting in the run-out, who had stamped out a waiting pad in the snow in the small rest area to stop for the sled and its entourage to pass by, providing an open path to the Eastern Ridge above. The hikers had already noticed the peculiarity of the sled with something tethered underneath the rainfly atop the wicker basket, as the rescue party approached the run-out. The accumulation of new snow on the trail made easy work for Dewey to negotiate the turn with the sled facing the opposite switchback, with Audrey providing necessary braking as he guided the backend of the sled around the turn. The hikers silently stared at the passing sled, and stood mesmerized as they observed the injured wolverine peering out from under the tent fly, as the rear of the sled passed their position. Dewey made good progress down the switchback towards the opposite run-out. The boy turned around to wave to the hikers and noticed that the small hiking party had remained transfixed at what they had seen. The boy began to sense new feelings of nervousness at the thought of having to give his account of their encounter with the timber wolves to his fellow students, teachers, and the authorities, who surely would be waiting for them upon their return home.

The boy's nervousness began to subside as the forest thinned during their descent, opening peek-a-boo glimpses of the valley below and the subtle outline of the more prominent buildings at the edge of the township. Before they knew it, the rescue party was passing across the small rock bridge that crossed Pinnacle Creek, marking the two-hundred-meter point before opening out into the trailhead where the boy and his grandfather had signed the back-country register only a few days earlier, providing the forest-service rangers with names and contact details of hikers venturing into the forest towards the Eastern Ridge. Unfortunately, during the winter months between November and February, the rangers seldom visited the trailhead until early spring; therefore, providing their details in the registry was more of a formality, unless the rangers were alerted of an emergency concerning travelers venturing into the forest.

Dewey covered the distance from the rock bridge to the opening into the trailhead in swift time.

The boy had expected to recognize only his grandfather's 1959 red and white Chevrolet Apache pickup truck, and Dewey's 1963 white Jeep Commando fit with the Smittybilt 97495 XRC Electric Winch, with its nine thousand-five hundred pounds load capacity, prominently fitted to the front chassis of the jeep, like a chrome bowsprit marking the fashionable lines of a well-maintained timber sailing sloop. He had not expected to be greeted by the thirty to forty well-wishers who had arrived from the township to meet the rescue party, with cars and SUVs, filling all of the available parking spaces in the small car park that terminated at the split-log timber fence mounted on half-height timber posts, protecting the trailhead and forest beyond from the possibility of intrusion by anything less than well-intentioned hikers into the forest.

The boy noticed his mother and grandmother emerge from the crowd that had assembled on the car-park side of the trailhead. Dr. Klein, who had been the veterinarian in the township for more years than the boy could remember, followed closely behind the boy's grandmother with his two assistants from his clinic, as the crowd opened to allow their passage. It was told that Dr. Klein had held the chief role as Head of Veterinary Medicine at the regional university in the city for many years, and had received numerous citations and commendations for his work, but following the tragic death of his wife, he had relocated to the small rural township upon his personal physician's advice to allow him to deal with the stress of his loss, and begin a new life. A few years after his move, he married a local woman who was also a widower, following the death of her husband after losing his fight with a terminal illness.

Dewey brought the sled to a stop a few meters from the split-log fence as the boy and his grandfather, along with

Audrey and Winston, remained standing guard around the injured wolverine, like sentinels protecting priceless cargo. Dr. Klein and his two assistants approached Grandfather, who turned and covered the few strides to the boy, who remained at the opening in the rainfly to the rear of the sled that exposed the wolverine, with Dr. Klein and his assistants following closely behind. Grandfather spoke a few quiet words to Dr. Klein, who motioned to the boy to kneel down in the snow facing the injured animal. Grandfather rolled back a section of the rainfly, exposing the wolverine's body, as Dr. Klein kneeled beside the boy in the snow, with the two of them looking passionately into the face of the injured animal. With the animal's body exposed, Grandfather noticed the large pool of blood that had dried underneath the wolverine. The boy glanced at his grandfather's face, and noticed his unwavering optimism and hope begin to fade as he peered at the pool of blood that had coagulated under the animal's body, and the numerous deep bite marks and injuries sustained from the timber wolves' vicious attack. The boy placed his left hand affectionately on the head of the wolverine, as Dr. Klein began to examine the injured animal. Grandfather and his hunting mates carefully observed Dr. Klein, following his hands that gently palpated the animals head, body, and legs, with his assistant recording his spoken notes during his physical examination of the animal's injuries. The animal flinched a few times when Dr. Klein, ever so gently, manipulated its legs, searching for any indications of deeper injury to tissue, muscle, and bone. The boy applied gentle pressure with his left hand on the wolverine's head during these times that seemed to comfort the animal from any pain and anxiety resulting from the physical examination.

In spite of what appeared to be his serious injuries that certainly would have paralyzed the strongest of animals, Grandfather and his hunting mates still considered the wolverine a wild animal, with a reputation that preceded him as a vicious and cunning predator, and remained captivated at the quiet composure the animal displayed during Dr. Klein's examination, with the boy's hand remaining on his head comforting him. Nevertheless, Grandfather had glanced over at Audrey who had silently raised his Remington Model-700 Springfield Rifle, and had it trained on the head of the wolverine, in the event the animal rallied enough strength to mount a defensive attack on Dr. Klein and the boy; however, the animal remained placate as though Dr. Klein had administered a strong sedative to relieve the injured animal of its pain. No sooner had Grandfather registered his thoughts of concern to himself than Dr. Klein quietly announced that he had completed his initial examination, and recommended that the wolverine be transported back to his clinic, where he and his assistants could further examine the animal by utilizing the specialized diagnostic equipment that the township had graciously gifted the clinic through generous charitable donations. Dr. Klein slowly turned to his assistant and quietly gave instructions to prepare a relatively strong sedative of Acepromazine that Dr. Klein typically used for dogs and larger animals. After searching for a viable vein on the animal's right leg, Dr. Klein gently administered the sedative with the remark that it would reduce the pain the animal was surely feeling, and begin to reduce the shock from the blood loss, providing comfort for the injured animal as they transported him to the clinic.

The boy remained with the wolverine, gently patting his head, as Grandfather, his hunting mates, Dr. Klein, and his two assistants lifted the sled with its patient still secured under the rainfly, onto the bed of Grandfather's Chevrolet Apache pickup truck for the drive back to the township and Dr. Klein's clinic.

The crowd that had assembled on the other side of the split-log fence separating the trail head from the car park, had remained surprisingly quiet, with whispers among one another as they observed the activity surrounding the patient secured to the sled. The men proceeded to Grandfather's pickup truck like pall-bearers, carrying a crudely fashioned casket for burial as the crowd quietly parted to either side, creating a single path to the back of the truck. As the sled with the injured wolverine passed by, the onlookers remained astonished to see the face of the animal appearing quite tranquil, with the boy's hand remaining on his patient's head providing comfort. Once the sled was lifted onto the open bed of the pickup truck, Grandfather and Dewey began to cover the animal once again with the rainfly, with Audrey and Winston taking up positions at the opposite side of the truck, as the men tethered the sledge to the bed of the truck with five-millimeter purloin accessory rope secured to the cleats welded to the top rim of the bed with a trucker's hitch.

Grandfather and the boy climbed into the cab of the Chevrolet Apache, as Dewey maneuvered his 1963 white Jeep Commando in front of Grandfather's Apache, to lead the convoy into the township and Dr. Klein's Clinic. Audrey and Winston were seated in the back cab of the Commando, where they had secured the rifles in the red gun rack mounted to the back of the cab, visible through the rear windscreen.

The crowd moved in unison to the back of Grandfather's truck, remaining engrossed with the injured wolverine under the rainfly that was no longer visible to the spectators. The atmosphere remained peculiarly silent throughout the crowd, with not a soul breaking rank, but the silence seemed to shroud the atmosphere with the thought of what was to become of the injured wolverine.

Chapter 11
Homeward Bound

*Home, for my heart still calls me; Home, through the
danger zone;*
Home, whatever befalls me, I will sail again to my own!

The drive to Dr. Klein's clinic in the middle of the township
was uneventful in comparison to the last two days the boy and
his grandfather had spent in the forest, surviving the attack by
the timber wolves from the Eastern Ridge. A light rain began
to fall with an accompanying dense fog rolling in across the
two-lane road, obscuring the view of Dewey's white
Commando leading the way to the clinic. Grandfather
engaged the old-style vacuum windshield wipers powered by
a manifold vacuum under the hood of the Apache that
Grandfather had never replaced, in spite of Mr. Kelly, the
townships sole automobile mechanic's plea to replace them
with the newer electric windshield wiper motors, at no cost.
The vacuum windshield wipers were not able to maintain a
constant, regular speed with their speed corresponding
directly with the speed of the engine, which didn't seem to
bother Grandfather in the slightest. Because the function of
the windshield wipers depended on the amount of vacuum
created in the engine, the wipers would stop working entirely
when the car was in a situation that lowered the pressure, such
as when Grandfather was trying to navigate up a steep hill.
The wipers would work in relation to the speed corresponding
directly with the speed of the engine. Fortunately, the terrain
of the road into the township was relatively smooth, providing
clear visibility to Dewey's white Commando that had begun
to become obscured in the dense fog and rain. The irregular

swish, swish, swish of the wiper blades across the windscreen, became hypnotizing to the boy as he peered out at the road in front as if in a trance.

The boy turned around to look at the bulge of the wolverine under the rainfly in the back of the Chevrolet's open bed. As he turned, he noticed Dr. Klein's 1966 green Jeep Wagoneer approaching and falling in line behind Grandfather's Apache. The convoy covered the five-kilometers to the clinic in about thirty minutes, with Dewey maintaining a slower speed to protect any adverse effects of the weather to the injured wolverine. The boy noticed that Dr. Klein's assistant sitting in the passenger side of the Wagoneer, was speaking into the two-way radio that Dr. Klein had installed in car. The boy suspected that the assistant was having a conversation with Dr. Klein's wife Roma at the clinic, to prepare for the arrival of their unusual patient.

Dr. Klein's veterinary clinic was known throughout the area as the Pinnacle Creek Animal Hospital, which had a more personalized name than a clinic. When Dr. Klein first moved into the township, he set up his practice in a converted photographic lab that didn't have enough room in the main entry lobby to swing a cat by its tail; however, Dr. Klein made do, and his skill as a diagnostician and veterinary surgeon became legendary, as animal owners in the township, and as far away as the larger city, booked appointments for Dr. Klein to treat their beloved pets. Many of the farmers in the adjoining acreages also began to call on Dr. Klein to treat their livestock, with assisting in the delivery of calves, colts, puppies, and kittens. One particular story had been shared at the local diner of Dr. Klein's emergency treatment of a cat that had presumably sustained a venomous snake bite, and Dr. Klein, taking the cat by the tail and gently swinging the cat in circles over his head like a rodeo rider swinging a lariat preparing to lasso a horse or cow, until the cat vomited the venom. The cat lay on the lawn as if dead for a few moments and then with little concern, staggered to its owner and curled up in her lap.

After Dr. Klein and his wife Roma married, they engaged an architect from the city, to design a major remodel of the old photographic lab, in order to provide a more modernized facility to service their customers and patients. The design of the main entry included a covered set-down area for cueing up to four to five vehicles, protecting owners and their patients from the rain and inclement weather. The main entry doors centered on the set-down portico, and led into a spacious lobby designed to maintain separation between cats and dogs waiting for treatment. Roma had assisted the architect in the design of attractive landscaping, bordering the main vehicle entry and car-parking area that personalized the design of the building, creating a warm and friendly approach to the hospital that both she and Dr. Klein had hoped would reduce the level of stress they believed their patients experienced when visiting Pinnacle Creek Animal Hospital. The main reception of the hospital was usually manned by Dr. Klein's two assistants, and stretched across the entire back wall of the lobby, restricting access to the two treatment rooms and two operating theaters located on either side of a wide access corridor, with a half-height, double-leafed lockable access gate. To the right off the main entry, the architect had designed a specialist trauma/triage room for emergency cases, with double external doors that opened onto a private emergency drive-through, along the side of the hospital building. The township had provided generous charitable donations on behalf of the hospital, to ensure it was equipped with the state-of-the-art diagnostic and treatment equipment, guaranteeing that Pinnacle Creek Animal Hospital remained an unprecedented facility throughout the region. Dr. Klein had used the donations wisely with the hospital, developing a very good reputation for providing high-quality care for its customers and pets. The hospital even extended its emergency services to the general public on occasion. During one summer, a frantic mother had arrived at the hospital with her fifteen-year-old son displaying the initial symptoms of anaphylactic shock, after he sustained multiple bee stings while mowing their back lawn. Roma ushered the mother and her son into the trauma room to the side of the main lobby, and quickly summoned Dr. Klein. A moment later, the doctor arrived with an EpiPen and administered an injection of epinephrine in the boy's arm in treating the allergic reaction. The mother and son left the hospital a short time later with Dr. Klein's instructions to schedule a follow-up checkup at the local hospital's emergency room.

The boy spotted Roma in her rain-gear, directing Dewey in his white Jeep Commando to proceed under the entry portico, and for Grandfather to turn into the emergency drive that passed along the side of the hospital building, stopping in front of the double doors opening into the trauma and emergency room. Dewey, Audrey, and Winston joined the boy and his grandfather, along with Dr. Klein and his assistants, as the men untied the purloin accessory ropes securing the sled to the cleats on the upper edge of the Chevrolet's bed, and began gently lifting the sled with the injured wolverine out of the bed of the truck onto the hardstand area adjacent to the doors. Dr. Klein motioned for Grandfather to remove the rainfly covering the animal, and motioned for the boy to gently place his hand on the head of the patient to provide comfort to the animal, although the wolverine appeared quite sedated following Dr. Klein administering the Acepromazine earlier at the trail head. With the exception of the boy who continued to comfort the animal, Dr. Klein motioned to Grandfather and his hunting mates, to step back from the sled as he and his assistants gently lifted the wolverine off the sled and onto a gurney or wheeled stretcher used for transporting injured or sedated animals within the hospital, that Roma had positioned at the foot of the sled.

The boy's eyes moved away from the wolverine's gaze while his hand remained on his head, as he noticed a newer-model white Toyota Land Cruiser pulling up behind his grandfather's Chevrolet Apache. Two middle-aged men stepped out of the vehicle and drew near to Dr. Klein and his assistants with the injured animal secured to the gurney. The boy noticed a sign on the Land Cruiser fixed to the driver's side door that read: *'Regional Veterinary University Research Laboratory.'* The boy had guessed that Dr. Klein had alerted his wife Roma to contact his close professional associates at the university, for assistance with the more involved physical examination of the injured wolverine, using the specialist diagnostic equipment in the hospital, taking advantage of his associates' expertise to collectively prepare an accurate diagnosis and effective treatment plan that he had hoped would save the animal's life, following his initial examination at the trail head that identified the seriousness of the wolverine's injuries.

Dr. Klein kindly motioned to the boy with a smile of compassion, to remove his hand now from the wolverine's head, as his assistants began moving the wheeled stretcher into the trauma/emergency room inside the hospital, with the two men from the university following closely behind the gurney. Dr. Klein dropped behind to speak with the boy and his grandfather and his hunting mates, to discreetly share with them the plan that he had formulated for his more detailed investigation and emergency treatment of the injured animal.

Dr. Klein truthfully told the men that the next forty-eight to seventy-two hours would be a critical time for administering effective emergency treatment to the wolverine, if he were to survive his injuries sustained from the timber wolves' attack. Dr. Klein explained in simple layman's terms the extent of the internal injuries to the animal, including the very deep injuries to deep tissue and bone. Dr. Klein also registered his surprise that the wolverine had actually survived such a vicious attack, and thus far had remained seemly stable, although the extent of his injuries was major that would require multiple surgeries to repair damaged tissue, bone, and internal organs. The boy began to understand the reputation Dr. Klein had developed with the residents of the township, and further afield to the larger city and throughout the region, and the legend that had been attributed to him, as the boy noticed tears welling up in Dr. Klein's eyes, reflecting the deep compassion and concern he held for his patient. He concluded his explanation of his treatment plan, and encouraged the men to return home but to maintain a steadfast vigil, since this would be a very long process, and the prognosis remained undetermined at the moment.

Dr. Klein turned and walked back through the double doors into the hospital's trauma/emergency room to join his associates and two assistants to begin their detailed examination of the wolverine's injuries, and draft an effective treatment plan. As the doors began to close on him, he shot a brief glance of unwavering hopefulness to the boy and his grandfather, and then disappeared into the hospital. The boy and his grandfather felt a thick and dreadful darkness come over them. Had their efforts to rescue and save the wolverine from the marauding timber wolves and their vicious attack, been completely unfruitful? Had they willingly put themselves in harm's way with the wolves, by believing a delusion that they could make any difference in the fate and survival of the wolverine? Perhaps they should have simply allowed nature to take its course without attempting to intervene. Grandfather's hunting mates sensed the dark dilemma that the boy and his grandfather were struggling with, as tears welled up in their eyes. The boy recognized that even with Grandfather's hardened hunting mates who had known and faced danger and death and the extremity of circumstances in the Alaskan wilderness, the character, resolve, and what appeared to be the unyielding determination to survive and live, deeply touched their emotions in a manner that was quite unfamiliar to them.

The boy's grandfather was the first to break the somber silence as he and the boy climbed into the cab of the Chevrolet Apache, and his hunting mates walked back to Dewey's white Jeep Commando that was parked in the entry portico of the hospital. The boy noticed that his grandfather's countenance had changed from sadness and hopelessness, to a similar resolve that the wolverine had displayed as he turned and said to the boy, "Have no fear of bad news, simply be still and believe, and wait patiently." These were perhaps the most pungent words of encouragement the boy had ever heard from his grandfather. The two of them remained quiet in their own thoughts, as Grandfather turned the Apache onto the main arterial, heading homeward bound, as the edges of the boy's mouth began to curl up, forming a very faint beam of strength, as he contemplated the steadfast vigil they would need to endure over the next number of days and weeks. Unbeknown to the boy and his grandfather, their steadfast vigil would last many weeks, as the winter months began to warm into spring with indicators of new life all around them.

Chapter 12
Safe at Last

Seas of sorrow, seas of trial, bitter anguish, fiercest pain;
Rolling surges of temptation, sweeping over heart and
brain...
Threatening breakers of destruction, doubt's insidious
undertow;
Will not sink us, will not drag us, out to ocean depths of woe.

The rain began to ease, changing to a heavy mist and fog that continued to obscure the road ahead, and Dewey's white Jeep Commando that led the convoy through the township towards home. Grandfather disengaged the vacuum-powered windshield wipers, and opened his window just a slit, allowing the air rushing into the cab to evaporate the condensation forming on the front windscreen. He also retrieved the old rag hidden from the boy's grandmother under the driver's seat, to assist in keeping the front windshield clear as the two of them remained silent in their own thoughts.

A few minutes later, Dewey waved to the boy and his grandfather from the driver side of the Commando, as the jeep veered to the left, heading up towards Dewey's home in Juanita Heights, at the edge of the township and the hinterland that led to the Western Escarpment. The days of the men's adventures in the Alaskan wilderness had come to a close a number of years earlier, when they began to suffer the afflictions of age with the onset of arthritis and stiff joints that limited their mobility. Grandfather, Audrey, and Winston had assumed a soothing and comfortable lifestyle in the township with their wives and families, giving up cold weather bivouacs on the side of a mountain, with the temperature plummeting below zero, and tolerating freeze-dried meals heated on an MSR wind-burner pressure-regulated stove system, in exchange for the comfort of their warm homes, sleeping on their Sealy Posturpedic Copper Mountain Beds, and enjoying an assortment of tasteful cuisines prepared by loving hands from well-equipped kitchens. Needless to say, the physiques of the three men reflected their indulgence in the joys of the 'good life', with slightly bulging mid-sections, challenges with controlling their blood sugar levels and blood pressure, and slower activity levels. For Grandfather, this amounted to moving from the comfort of his bed to the dining table to enjoy breakfast between 9:00 a.m. to 10:00 a.m. on Saturday mornings, and then moving to the sofa to enjoy his customary cigar, much to Grandmother's protests, and then back to his bed for his morning nap. Audrey and Winston had assumed a similar lifestyle with their families close by, and the squeals and activity of small grandchildren underfoot.

Dewey had never remarried after his wife abandoned him, and moved to the city where she married a lawyer who had a thriving law practice, and could afford to fund her extravagant lifestyle that had been lost on a man who enjoyed the wilderness and the spectacle of watching an early-morning sunrise at ten thousand feet, and the sun turning everything to vibrant pink as it pushed its way up through the lower-level cloud layer. Dewey and his ex-wife never had any children of their own, that allowed him to thoroughly enjoy his mate's children and grandchildren on a limited and convenient basis. However, Dewey, and Grandfather had been much closer with one another than with their other mates, and Dewey had become very fond of the boy, often taking him aside to share with him the exploits, bravery, and endearing qualities of the boy's grandfather.

Unlike Grandfather, Audrey, and Winston, Dewey continued to maintain a rigorous schedule of activity that typically began early every morning around 4:30 a.m., when he spent up to an hour reading his Bible and devotions, and then going into the hinterland behind his home on what he called his prayer walks. Unlike his hunting mates, Dewey retained an athletic and strong physique that he attributed to his regular activity level, his participation in the senior's aqua-aerobics at the local pool three times each week, and his special Asian diet prepared by his Chinese housekeeper, Xiao Xue, whom he had brought home with him from Jilin City in Northeastern China. Dewey had attempted to teach Xiao Xue to speak limited English, and he had tried to learn some Mandarin; however, both of them had failed miserably in these endeavors. Nevertheless, they had developed a unique communication system that over the years allowed them to understand what the other was thinking or saying without actually understanding each other's native language.

As Grandfather approached the house, the boy realized how hungry he was and how famished Grandfather must have been, having no food throughout the ordeal with the timber wolves and the descent to the trail head, nibbling only on a scone that Grandmother had prepared and handed to him at the trail head. The boy had also begun to realize the effects that the stress of the trial was having on his mind and body as he slumped down in the passenger side of the Apache. Grandfather turned into the driveway that had been remodeled the year before to provide space for four vehicles on either side with a turn out that allowed the driver to turn the car around in the drive without having to back out into traffic.

Before Grandfather had brought the Apache to a stop in the driveway, Grandmother and the boy's mother were at the doors of the truck, helping the men out of the cab and into the warmth and comfort of the kitchen's breakfast area that seated up to six around a medium-sized oblong cedar dining table located off to the right of the kitchen corridor, adjacent to the kitchen's serving counters. The sight of the hearty meal that the women had prepared and laid out for the boy and his grandfather, was lost on his thoughts for the welfare of the injured wolverine that filled his mind and imagination. The boy and his grandfather shared the meal with his grandmother and mother in virtual silence, with the women mindful of the incredible ordeal the two of them had been through. After finishing most of the meal, the women helped the boy and his grandfather to their own bedrooms upstairs, with both of them quickly falling into a deep sleep.

Chapter 13
A Steadfast Vigil

My eyes were steadfastly toward the wall; while impatience surely took its toll,
My faith was challenged day by day, with little good I came to say;
Impatient waiting my dark impasse, but my faith prevailed until at last,
My goal achieved, my heart rejoiced, the victory my soul did voice.

The boy opened his eyes to the morning sun streaming in through his bedroom window, with his mother having drawn the window blinds earlier that morning while the boy remained sleeping, oblivious to his mother's activity in his bedroom. He lay quietly under his bedcovers, looking out through the bedroom window at the old maple tree that had grown up over the years, with the gentle spring breeze causing the leaves to dance on their limbs, creating a strobe light effect on the walls of his bedroom with the sunshine filtering through. He began to dwell on the timber wolves' attack once again, the descent to the trail head, and the many well-wishers who had driven out from the township to meet the rescue party, whom he had spoken with over the last number of weeks. His thoughts quickly changed to feelings of anguish and concern as he considered the continuing condition and wellbeing of the wolverine.

His steadfast vigil had merged from days into weeks as every day he rode his bike to the Pinnacle Creek Animal Hospital after school during the week and in the early mornings over the weekends. Dr. Klein had quickly recognized the unusual bond that had formed between the boy and the wolverine, and his patient's stirrings in his enclosure at the sound of the boy entering the hospital lobby during his daily visits. Dr. Klein had explained to the boy in simple words the extent of the injuries the wolverine had suffered during the vicious attack by the wolves. He had also shared with him, as best he could, the proposed treatment plan that he and his associates from the university had agreed, and that the element of time remained the determining factor for success of the treatment along with the wolverine's resolve to heal. The boy observed that Dr. Klein's associates from the university frequently visited the hospital and the patient, remarking on the miraculous recovery the animal seemed to be making in light of its serious injuries. Dr. Burke had become particularly interested in the case, making the forty-five-minute drive from the university to the hospital a few times each week. Grandfather had suggested that the boy begin to talk to the wolverine in a gentle voice as a means of providing comfort, reassuring the convalescing animal of its safety, and the boy's care and friendship. Surprisingly, Dr. Klein and Dr. Burke noticed that this appeared to make a difference in the animal's behavior and its level of activity in its limited surroundings during the boy's visits. So the boy began to enjoy the conversations of friendship they shared together, although it remained quite one-sided with the boy's monolog recounting the events of the day at school and plans he conceived for the two of them, including his grandfather and Dewey, on expeditions into the wilderness after the wolverine had fully recovered.

The wolverine's fur had grown back over the multiple sites on its body where the doctors had surgically repaired muscle, bone, and internal injuries. Dr. Klein had splinted the animal's front right leg and rear left leg where the bone had been seriously damaged by the powerful jaws of the wolves. Dr. Burke had followed the boy into the hospital this morning, joining Dr. Klein in his office as the boy made his way to the wolverine's enclosure. Dr. Klein's wife Roma greeted the boy in her customary fashion, noting that his regular daily visits appeared to be wearing a permanent path across the honed marble tiling in the entry lobby and the patterned vinyl composite floor tiling in the corridor that led to the wolverine's special enclosure. A few moments after Dr. Burke's arrival, and as he had joined Dr. Klein, the doctors heard the boy calling out, asking if the wolverine was supposed to be standing and moving about its enclosure. In an instant, the two doctors were standing outside the enclosure, gazing at the remarkable sight of their patient slowly moving about on all four legs, gently rubbing up against the boy's legs in an endearing act of affection. Dr. Klein replied with a tinge of joy in his voice that it was perfectly alright for the animal to move about; however, the boy should gently encourage only short circumnavigations of its enclosure. The next day, Dr. Klein contacted a specialist contractor from the city named Nature Scapes, who specialized in the design and construction of wildlife exhibits and enclosures, to construct an indoor/ outdoor area for the wolverine across the back of the hospital adjacent to the animal kennels. Plans were drawn up and the next week, David Joffee and his wife Kathryn arrived with their two laborers at the hospital in their two Dodge Ram 4500 HD Flatbed Landscape Trucks, loaded with an assortment of boulders, timber stumps, fallen logs retrieved from the forest, and containers of rock, sand, and cement. As Dr. Klein greeted Mr. Joffee, his attention was turned to two more work trucks pulling up behind the landscape flatbeds, displaying the sign *'Levine's Plumbing'* fixed to the driver-side doors. Moshe Levine had undertaken the plumbing works for the major remodel of the Pinnacle Creek Animal Hospital, and appeared to have been engaged by David Joffee to undertake the proposed plumbing works for the construction of the wolverine's special enclosure. Mr. Levine was a tall man with a very large frame, who maintained a long black beard even throughout the warmer months, when he was often found under the buildings or in attic spaces, installing pipework or ductwork for his projects. He stepped from the cab of his truck and covered the short distance to where Mr. Joffee and Dr. Klein were standing, in a few long strides with a set of drawings rolled up under his right arm.

Over the next few weeks, an attractive enclosure was constructed for the wolverine's more permanent home, with boulders assembled to replicate the animal's natural habitat in the forest at the base of the Eastern Ridge. The enclosure included a small rock cave constructed at one end of the area that abutted the back-exterior wall of the hospital, providing shelter from inclement weather. A much smaller open internal enclosure had also been constructed inside the hospital in the kennel area that abutted the rock cave with a clear Plexiglas hinged door, separating the external run from the internal enclosure but still allowing for views of the wolverine outside. The internal enclosure allowed Dr. Klein and his associates to perform examinations and administer treatment of the recovering animal while remaining within the hospital.

The length of the run included tree stumps and sections of fallen trees that Mr. Joffee's team had positioned and secured strategically to imitate the area surrounding the wolverine's home in the forest. Mr. Levine and his team had constructed a small running creek along one side of the enclosure that extended from the rock cave, along the entire length of the run that connected to the potable water system of the hospital. Mr. Levine had installed a recycling pumping system that discharged the water from a concealed pipe within the external wall of the cave into the streambed, and recycled the water back to the pumping system from the end of the water course. News of the special works was spread by word of mouth through the township and as far away as the larger city. The local newspaper began publishing articles reporting the progress of the works with black and white photographs accompanying the articles.

Most of the students at school had begun associating the boy as the 'Wolverine Boy', with his involvement in the rescue of the wolverine from the forest and his steadfast vigil and the close bond that had developed between the boy and the animal. The boy's encounter with the timber wolves and his survival from their vicious attack became a familiar story, and eventually a legend amongst his classmates. Over the weeks and months that followed during the boy's steadfast vigil, he was asked to share his story with different classes in school. His feelings of being humiliated and embarrassed by his classmates quickly changed as he was credited with unprecedented bravery in mounting his stand against the wolves, and his reputation spread throughout the school as a role model to fellow students who had also been subjected to verbal abuse and indignation by the more popular students.

Construction of the wolverine's special enclosure was nearing completion. Mr. Joffee had commissioned an artist from the city to create a diorama across the full length of the rear wall of the enclosure, denoting a partially three-dimensional, full-size replica or scale model of the wolverine's natural habitat. A few of the teachers from the boy's school arranged with Dr. Klein to inspect the nearly completed enclosure and the much-talked-about diorama. The teachers were extremely impressed with the level of detail, accuracy, and effort that all of the workers had rendered in the construction of the enclosure, and recommended to the school's principal and board of education that the wolverine in its protective habitat of its specially built enclosure, be used for the purpose of education with any charitable proceeds gifted to Dr. Klein and his wife Roma for the regular maintenance and care of the animal. The recommendation was unanimously approved, with the principal and board members excited with the prospect of being able to provide a unique learning tool to help show students an understanding of what had for so long been considered to be a ferocious North American carnivore, that had a reputation for hunting as a solitary predator, seldom seen because of its crafty and cunning character.

The weekend after the wolverine's enclosure had been commissioned, Dr. Klein arranged for Dr. Burke, along with Dewey, Audrey, Winston, and the boy with his grandfather to attend a special ceremony commemorating the enclosure as Dr. Klein, Dr. Burke, and the boy, prepared to move the wolverine into his new home. Dr. Klein had removed the splints from the animal's legs weeks earlier, with the wolverine's activity level that seemed to increase when the boy was present, limited by the smaller treatment enclosure that had been home to the animal during the months of treatment and rehabilitation. Dr. Klein and Dr. Burke were both satisfied that the animal had recovered sufficiently, and that relocating their patient into an environment that was more aligned with its natural habitat, would promote the animal's further healing and strengthening that was required.

The wolverine obediently followed the boy into the cave, with the boy exiting out the other side into the open area of the enclosure. Grandfather and his hunting mates stood in silence along the outside of the animal's new home that was protected with a medium gauge green-colored PVC chain link fence, waiting for the animal to follow the boy into the open area; however, the animal remained in its cave, peering out into the open area, while the boy gently encouraged his friend to follow. Grandfather slowly leaned towards Dewey, quietly voicing his concerns that perhaps the authenticity of the enclosure, particularly the diorama across the back wall, may rekindle memories of fear that could traumatize the wolverine. Dewey turned to Grandfather and uttered a quiet reply, "Just believe."

The boy took up a position seated on one of the smaller boulders halfway to the end of the run that retained the streamlet flowing to the end of the water course, and then silently recirculating back to the discharge pump located outside the cave to repeat its flow. The boy remained silent as he watched movement inside the cave, and then the wolverine cautiously emerging from the cave, and slowly walking to the boy as he affectionately rubbed up against the boy's legs in an obvious sign of affection. The boy sensed that his steadfast vigil had at last come to an end, as feelings of emotion choked his voice and tears began to well up in his eyes. As he glanced around at the doctors and his grandfather and hunting mates, he saw that he was not alone in his emotions.

Chapter 14
New Beginnings

Eccl. 7:3 – "Sorrow is better than laughter, because a sad face is good for the heart. It takes sorrow to expand and deepen the soul."

Summer merged into fall, with the leaves on the old maple outside the boy's bedroom transforming from green to red, orange, and then yellow, eventually falling from their branches and creating a natural carpet on the lawn below. The days began to become shorter with the sun shining less, as fall changed into winter and the township recorded its first light snowfall.

The wolverine had adjusted well to its new habitat, and as Dr. Klein and Dr. Burke had hoped, the natural environment and increasing time in the outside open area of the enclosure, noticeably strengthened the animal, promoting rapid healing from its remaining injuries. The boy had continued his daily visits with the wolverine, Dr. Klein, and his wife Roma, as they observed the close relationship and bond of love that had developed between the boy and his mate over the many months they had spent together.

The local school had made good on its commitment, along with public and private schools in the city that had taken advantage of the invitation to visit the wolverine in its replicated habitat as a learning tool for students, that generated more than sufficient income for Dr. Klein and his wife Roma to comfortably maintain the enclosure and provide a special diet for the wolverine's wellbeing. Dr. Klein and Dr. Burke began to observe that the wolverine had become more active within its special enclosure, and agreed that it was time to introduce the wolverine to the environment outside. The boy arrived after school on a Friday afternoon and was greeted by Dr. Klein, Dr. Burke, and Dr. Klein's wife Roma, as he entered the hospital lobby. Dr. Klein moved towards the boy and presented him with a giftwrapped box, and motioned with a guarded smile for the boy to open the box. The boy quickly removed the giftwrapping and opened the box with curious excitement, revealing an adjustable black nylon-webbed animal harness with a lead about two meters long, with a trendy stitched hand loop at the one end of the lead and a small locking carabineer at the opposite end that clipped to a stainless-steel eyelet stitched into the top side of the webbing that fit around the animal's shoulders and upper body. The harness was equipped with a velvet lining at the position where the harness fit behind the animal's front legs to provide comfort. The boy silently stared at the harness for a few moments, until the doctor's implied objective dawned on him. Looking up towards Dr. Klein, his only response was, "Really?"

The first excursions outside the wolverine's enclosure were around the hospital building with Dr. Klein and Dr. Burke following a few meters behind to provide assistance if needed. The boy had fit the animal harness to the wolverine and adjusted the webbing to snugly but not uncomfortably tight. The pair moved together with the boy, allowing plenty of slack in the lead, permitting the animal to move freely as they covered a few meters before the wolverine stopped and glanced behind him to examine where they had come from. The two of them repeated this pattern until they had moved around the building along the green PVC cyclone fencing outside the wolverine's enclosure. The animal moved a few steps along the side of the watercourse and then stopped, raising its head and sniffing the air. The wolverine repeated this pattern every few steps, recognizing the enclosure and the smells of his habitat. Dr. Klein limited the boy and the wolverine's circumnavigation of the hospital building to four trips every other day the first week, careful not to subject the wolverine to too much stimuli outside its enclosure, and unnecessarily tire the animal. However, his patient continued to display increasing strength over the first week of their ventures around the hospital, much to the satisfaction of Dr. Klein.

After successfully completing four weeks of their ventures around the hospital with no apparent harmful impact to the wolverine's recovery, Dr. Klein agreed to Grandfather's suggestion, that they introduce the wolverine to his natural environment, by allowing the boy to walk the wolverine along a section of the widened trail in the hinterland at the base of the Western Escarpment, where Dewey made his early-morning prayer walks each day.

The boy rode with Dewey in his white Jeep Commando with the wolverine comfortably contained in a meshed cage used for transporting larger animals that had been secured to the tie-down bolts in the back of the jeep. Audrey and Winston rode with Grandfather in his Chevrolet Apache, with Dr. Klein and Dr. Burke following the convoy in Dr. Burke's white Land Cruiser. The trucks followed a widened fire trail cleared in the underbrush that led to the start of the hinterland trail, only large enough to allow single-file passage by an off-road vehicle for about five hundred meters up a steepening grade to the start of the trail. The fire trail was used by the National Park's service rangers to access the hinterland trail and the Western Escarpment above. The widened fire trail appeared only on the National Forestry Maps, with access by the general public prohibited. However, few people in the township were aware that the fire trail and hinterland trail existed. Dewey had been held in high esteem by his hunting mates as an expert in orienteering and had only discovered the widened trail and adjoining hinterland trail purely by accident, as he descended the Western Escarpment through the hinterland via a new route a few years earlier. Crusted snow had remained on either side of the widened trail, hindering the vehicles' progress if they veered from the center of the path. The steepening grade compounded the difficulty for the vehicles' progress to the start of the hinterland trail. Grandfather had driven as far as he was comfortable in 2WD. He stopped the Apache, placing the transmission in neutral, engaging the emergency foot brake, and climbing down out of the cab. He began manually turning the hubs on the individual wheels to engage the 4WD system to safely continue the drive up to the hinterland trail.

The boy looked back at the wolverine every few minutes to ensure he was comfortable and reassured him of his presence as they made their way up the rough terrain of the widened fire trail. They finally reached the end of the trail that opened out into the hinterland trail. Unlike the trail head to the Eastern Ridge, there was no parking area or even a turnout to maneuver the trucks or back around to face the opposite direction down the trail. Dewey assisted the boy in securing the animal harness around the wolverine, and moving him out of the Commando to the front of the jeep onto the trail.

As the boy and the wolverine started down the hinterland trail, the animal repeated the same pattern he had displayed venturing around the hospital building, walking a few meters and then stopping to peer behind him to see where he had come from; however, as the two of them pushed further down the trail, the wolverine began slowly veering off the trail into the underbrush, with the boy having to give a gentle tug on the lead connected to the animal harness to encourage the animal back onto the trail. Grandfather and his hunting mates, including Dr. Klein, immediately recognized what the wolverine was doing, with faint tears clouding their eyes as they recognized the fate of the deep relationship and bond of affection that had grown between the boy and the wolverine.

Grandfather and the boy continued their journeys to the hinterland trail over the next few months on Saturday mornings, with Dewey in his Jeep Commando and the wolverine sitting next to the boy on the back bench seat comfortably restrained in its harness. The winter gradually changed to spring with the widened fire trail free of snow and the newly grown wild grass providing added traction for the Commando's climb to the hinterland trail.

Dewey intentionally lay back as the boy and his grandfather, with the wolverine leading the three of them, continued down the trail together one Saturday morning in April, opening up the distance between them. Dewey and the boy's grandfather had talked and prayed over this moment for weeks, hoping the boy would understand what he eventually would be called to do, and that he would be brave enough to overcome the sadness and loss he would be subjected to by his faithful resolve. Everyone who had been involved with the rescue and rehabilitation of the wolverine recognized the deep and tender feelings of affection and kindness the boy openly showed to the animal, arising from the kinship and a sense of underlying oneness they shared. The boy had formed an intense emotional attachment for his friend that would give birth to a time of deep darkness, sadness, and loss as the fate of their relationship moved to its final episode. Grandfather had gently shared with the boy that if you love something, you must let it go. If it comes back to you, then it's yours forever. If it doesn't, then it was never meant to be. The boy quietly pondered the words his grandfather shared with him. His grandfather explained that by turning the other person loose, if they come back, which is really what you want, it's because they love you and the feeling is mutual. However, if they don't come back, you would have only been fighting a losing battle to hold on to them, which is a battle you will eventually lose. The boy once again silently pondered his grandfather's words, and remained quiet as the three of them rounded a turn in the trail that opened to an alpine meadow painted on the steep slopes with a carpet of red columbine, common paintbrush, yarrow, and fragrant white and purple crocus. The meadow was bordered either side by a stand of Douglas fir and pines that rose to the base of the Western Escarpment above.

The boy began to recognize the gentle encouragement that his grandfather, Dr. Klein, and Dewey had shared with him over the last number of weeks, preparing him for this moment, even arranging the recovery treks along the hinterland trail weeks earlier, gently hiking around the base of the Western Escarpment far from the marauding Eastern Ridge timber wolves, that had been a loving choice by the men. This time, the boy stopped, bringing the three of them to a halt alongside the alpine meadow. He scanned the carpet of wildflowers that rose on the steep slope, and closing his eyes, smelled the fragrant hint of the crocus and cedar on the light breeze wafting down from the Western Escarpment. Glancing up to the escarpment, he watched the spring breeze blowing the last of a light overnight snow dusting over the ridge being carried upward on the currents of the breeze. His thoughts of the beauty and peace of this place caused either side of his mouth to gently roll up into a subtle but joyful smile. He moved with the wolverine down the trail until they were in front of the stand of fir and pines that bordered the meadow. Closing his eyes, he listened to the gentle voice of the wind as it softly blew through the outstretched limbs of the trees. He began to feel an emptiness in the pit of his stomach as he contemplated his circumstances and the fate of his relationship with his friend. Opening his eyes, he slowly bent down, unclipped the leash from the stainless-steel eyelet attached to the top section of webbing, and removed the harness from the wolverine. The two of them stood in the middle of the trail staring at each other, searching for some reassurance that the affection and love they felt for each other that had grown over the many months together, could overcome any trial of separation. A Steller's jay, with its striking deep blue and black plumage and shaggy crest, caught the wolverine's attention as the bird darted between the wildflowers, coming to rest on the gnarled limp of an old cedar log that had once belonged to a majestic tree that had been fallen by the blast of a winter storm years earlier. The wolverine veered off the trail into the underbrush that had become his pattern during their walks, stopping a few meters from the jay and scanning the upper sections of the alpine field and either side of the stand of fir and pine bordering the meadow. The wolverine ventured another few meters up the steep slope of the meadow and turned around peering back at the boy for his reassurance. The boy continued to stare back at the animal as tears welled up in his eyes and began trickling down his cheeks. The boy wiped his tears away with the sleeve of his jumper, and looked back at the wolverine who was still peering at the boy. The boy slowly raised his right hand and replied to the unseen emotion flowing between the two of them, "It's OK".

The wolverine stood staring at the boy for a few more minutes, and then turned, facing the Western Escarpment above, and quickly ran to the top of the meadow with its distinctive gait and disappeared into the stand of trees. The boy remained motionless, remembering his Grandfather's words, *If it comes back to you, then it's yours forever. If it doesn't, then it was never meant to be.* After a few more minutes, Grandfather lovingly placed his hand on the boy's right shoulder, motioning to him that it was time to return to the car and go home.

That night, the boy's sleep was fitful with his concern for the wolverine's welfare alone in the wilderness. His pillow was soaked from the tears he had cried following the release of the animal back into its natural habitat. He rose early the next morning and rode to the animal hospital where Dr. Klein's wife Roma was attending to early appointments, leading the animal and their owners into the trauma/emergency room for Dr. Klein's initial examination. Roma glanced at the boy with a loving look of approval as the boy made his way to the rear of the hospital, and the door that opened into the internal section of the wolverine's enclosure. The boy opened the door, and stooping down, entered the cave and exited into the open outside section of the enclosure. The watercourse was still gently flowing as the boy listened to the sounds of the water flowing over the rocks and boulders that

Mr. Joffee and Mr. Levine had constructed. He sat down on his favorite boulder, remembering how the wolverine would affectionately rub up against his leg, even with the splints on his legs. The boy thought back over the many events and circumstances the two of them had shared over the last year, from the initial discovery of the wolverine lying injured in the ravine following the attack by the timber wolves, to the encounter with the timber wolves on the Pinnacle, and then the many weeks and months of his steadfast vigil watching the wolverine convalesce and recover. A small grin formed on the boy's face as he began to realize that something had changed in himself, and that he had learned to love and exercise faith through the heart and life of what legend had reported to be a ferocious carnivore, that hunts as a solitary predator, seldom seen because of its crafty and cunning character.

Epilogue

*They tell me that I must bruise the rose's leaf, 'ere I can
keep and use its fragrance brief;
They tell me I must break the skylark's heart, 'ere her cage
song will make the silence start;
They tell me love must bleed, and friendship weep, 'ere in
my deepest need I touch that deep.
Must it be always so with precious things? Must they be
bruised and go with beaten wings?
Ah, yes! By crushing days, by caging nights, by scar; of
thorn and
stony ways these blessings are!*

The heat of the summer sun warmed the outstretched branches of the cedars, releasing the distinctive fragrance of its needles into the gentle breeze wafting down from the Western Escarpment above. Dewey stopped in the middle of the hinterland trail during his morning's prayer walk. Closing his eyes, he listened to the gentle breeze blowing through the branches of the stand of trees off the trail. He opened his eyes to the sound of human voices from down the trail but still out of view. A few moments later, he greeted two forest-service rangers rounding the bend in the trail as they approached him. Dewey offered the rangers a seat for a moment's rest on top of the old fallen log lying on the side of the trail where it had toppled years earlier. The rangers recognized the retired Alaskan hunting guide from the township where his reputation preceded him. They also remembered his participation in the rescue of the wolverine that had survived the timber wolves' attack and its long recovery, noting that the local newspaper had identified the members of the rescue party with their photos mounted across the front page of the first editions reporting on the rescue. The one ranger also recounted the violation citation the National Park Service had served on Dewey for unlawfully discharging a firearm in a national park, that had never been enforced following the submission of a petition signed by the senior members of the township's local counsel, appealing for leniency on Dewey's behalf in consideration of the unique and dangerous circumstances that he helped to diffuse. One ranger motioned to his partner that they should keep moving so they could return to their Forest Service Chevrolet Suburban 4WD Sport Utility parked at the base of the widened fire trail before nightfall. As the rangers started down the trail, that ranger turned back to face Dewey and informed him that on a number of their recent inspections into the forest, and along the Western Escarpment, they had observed a family of wolverines that included a large male, a female, and three kits. The ranger told Dewey that the larger wolverine displayed an unusual behavior, especially in the presence of humans, where fearlessly he sided up to the rangers and began rubbing against their legs in what seemed to be a show of affection. The ranger turned and joined his partner as they continued down the trail. Dewey rose from his seat on the old log, and standing in the center of the trail, raised his arms and hands in a gesture of thanks as a huge smile formed across his face.

Grandfather motioned for Dewey to take a seat in one of the handcrafted cedar chairs around the oblong cedar table in the kitchen's breakfast area, as the remainder of the family arrived from the upstairs bedrooms for breakfast. The table had been hewn from two cedar logs cut from sections of a majestic old cedar that had been toppled, roots and all, during a wild winter storm that had devastated large areas of the forest at the base of the Eastern Ridge. The tree had been blown over facing directly up hill, testifying to the immense power of the wind, straddling three of the switchbacks blocking all access along the trail. Grandfather and Dewey, along with a few other athletic and able-bodied men from the township, had been enlisted by the National Park Service to assist the rangers in clearing the trail of debris and fallen timber and repairing the damaged sections of the switchbacks. Grandfather and Dewey had arrived at the trail head on the appointed morning with Dewey's MS 880 STIHL Magnum Chainsaw, fit with a forty-eight-inch guide bar and three spare tungsten carbide guide chains. Grandfather brought his pro-universal double-headed forestry ax with its custom-fabricated hickory handle. Both sides of the ax had been engraved with *'U.S. Forest Service'* on either side of the forged steel double head that brought a suspicious grin to the face of the rangers. Following a full weekend of clearing debris and repairing the trail, Dewey asked the rangers if he could retrieve the two large sections of the cedar log that had been cut to open up the trail. The next weekend, Grandfather and Dewey transported the two cedar sections to a local fine furniture craftsman, who spent two months hewing the two sections of the table, and then laminating them to construct the one-of-a-kind table that now sat in the breakfast area in the kitchen.

Grandmother and the boy's mother placed a plate piled high with quarter-inch thick bacon rashers, scrambled eggs covered in a warm porcelain chafing dish, steaming fried potatoes on a serving platter, and an assortment of cold and hot drinks on to the cedar table. The family considered Dewey part of the family, with everyone catching up on their latest news as they enjoyed breakfast together. The boy and his grandfather, along with Dewey, remained at the table as the rest of the family finished the meal and either moved to the kitchen to clean up or left the kitchen to assume other Saturday activities. The boy had recently celebrated his seventeenth birthday, and thanked Dewey for the extravagant gift of the pair of Asolo TPS 520-GV hiking boots, perhaps the best boots available on the market. Dewey began to share with the boy and his grandfather his recent encounter with the park rangers on the hinterland trail during his prayer walk earlier in the week. Dewey gave an account of the park rangers' sighting of the family of wolverines halfway up the trail to the Western Escarpment that included a large male, a female, and three young kits. The boy slowly set his hot drink on the table as his eyes fixed on Dewey's, and offered a simple single-word of reply, "Really?" Dewey and Grandfather both smiled. Dewey paused for a few moments and then continued relating the rangers' account of how the male wolverine displayed an unusual behavior, bravely siding up to the rangers and rubbing up against their legs in what seemed to be a show of affection. The boy remained motionless as the deeper meaning of Dewey's account of the rangers' report began to well up inside him with joy he had not felt for some time. The boy clasped his hands together and slowly bowed his head towards the table as a huge smile beamed across his face. The three men remained silent as they contemplated the news that Dewey had brought. The boy broke the silence when he looked up into Dewey's face, with tears of joy trickling down his cheeks. The boy's only words to Dewey were, "Thank you."

I'm going by the upper road, for that still holds the sun,
I'm climbing through night's pastures where the starry
rivers run,
If you should think to seek me in my old dark abode,
You'll find this writing on the door, "He's on the upper
road."